THE DRAFT DODGER

To Geneviève:
May your innocence
always balance the sadness of men
L.C.

for Sheila Fischman
D.T.H.

THE DRAFT DODGER

LOUIS CARON

ANANSI 🕷   TORONTO

The characters in this novel are creations of the imagination;
history and geography have been respected as much as possible.

Cover design: Joss Maclennan

Originally published in French as *L'Emmitouflé*
© Editions Robert Laffont, Paris 1977

Translated with the assistance of the Canada Council. Published with
assistance from the Ontario Arts Council and the Canada Council.

Made in Canada for
House of Anansi Press Limited
35 Britain Street
Toronto, Ontario M5A 1R7

Canadian Cataloguing in Publication Data

Caron, Louis, 1942-
[L'emmitouflé. English]
The draft dodger

(Anansi fiction series ; AF 42)
Translation of L'emmitouflé.

ISBN 0-88784-085-X pa.

I. Title. II. Title: L'emmitouflé. English.

PS8555.A76E4413   C843'.54   C80-094769-X
PQ3919.2.C37E4413

Printed and bound in Canada by
T. H. Best Printing Company Limited, Don Mills, Ontario

CONTENTS

Translator's Note

During the preparation of the translation of *L'Emmitouflé*, the author took the opportunity to make certain changes in his novel. These have been incorporated in this version.

D.T.H.

PROLOGUE

When Sammy's battered pick-up stopped in the yard at my sister's place near Lowell, back home in Vermont, it was around eleven at night. No lights. Everybody was sleeping, I guess. As usual, the big Sentinel floodlight lit the lawn and part of the house.

I said to Sammy, "We'll have to wake them up."

He hesitated. "I don't know," he said. "Maybe we should sleep in the pick-up instead. I've got a big tarp, we could cover ourselves with that."

I looked at him. He looked even darker than he was during the day, with his big eyes shining in the light of the Sentinel.

"You and your black ideas," I said. "You've got to stop being afraid of everything. We're at my sister's place. If I brought you here, that means there's no danger. My sister will treat us like kings, you'll see. Come on!"

I gave him a push toward the porch. We knocked three or four times, then a light came on in the window of the upstairs front room. A minute later the door opened and there she was, my sister Françoise, her hair all messed up, one hand holding her housecoat, the other leaning on the door frame. She looked me right in the eye. She glanced at Sammy too, then she said, "Hey, it's my little brother! What are you doing showing up like this in the middle of the night? Well, come on in, we're not going to spend the rest of the night outside."

We went into the house and Sammy followed. My sister turned on the big fluorescent light in the kitchen, then we sat down around the table. Everything was ready for breakfast, the plates, cups and cereal boxes in the middle.

With a nod in his direction, I said, "That's Sammy. He was with me in Montreal. He doesn't look like much but his ideas are brighter than his skin, I guarantee it."

Sammy laughed. My sister asked, "Where are you going anyway?"

"Here, that's where!" I answered. "You don't think I've travelled enough as it is? Mexico and Canada, five years on the road, don't you think that's enough?"

She looked at both of us.

"You didn't get into trouble, did you?"

"We're as pure as new-driven snow," I said.

We turned to Sammy and all three of us burst out laughing. Then my sister made us something to eat, toast, honey, peanut butter and coffee. We ate like there was no tomorrow. Afterward we each lit up a cigarette, and I tilted my chair back on two legs.

I said, "Let me tell you, there's nothing like running and hiding for five years to make you feel like getting somewhere. Understand what I mean? I'm the same as before, only I'm sick of being far from home. If that sounds stupid, it is. A man needs a place of his own, that's for sure!"

Françoise had her elbows on the table and was looking at me without moving. Sammy nodded yes. There was silence for a minute and I went on.

"I'm going to tell you something. You might not know it, but your little brother almost became a hero, like in the movies. A hero in spite of himself, I mean. When I'm finished telling you, you'll see why I came back."

I gave Françoise another look. She lit herself a cigarette too, but she didn't loosen the good grip she had on her house-coat. She bent her head as she listened to me and I saw she had grey hair. Not a lot, some grey threads here and there. But we're

8

fifteen years apart. She bent her head and the smoke from her cigarette made her close her eyes.

"You remember what Dad said when I left? He said, You, boy, either you're about to make a fool out of yourself and it's going to turn out bad, or else the rest of the world is going to change and they'll see you were the one who was right. He told me that, then he didn't say another word to me during the three days I was at the house before I left. I ran away, I went to Mexico but there was nothing to do there. I even went to the Cuban embassy. They told me they could get me a tourist visa, nothing more. I was ready to ask for asylum in Cuba. In those days I didn't know what I know today. I came back fast enough, but when I got here, to the States, I was afraid, Françoise, I was afraid, you don't know what it's like. The first guy I saw standing on the corner lighting a cigarette, looking in my direction, I was sure he was an FBI agent. I was afraid, I travelled at night, on the bus, and I didn't dare stop here because I told myself they must be watching the house. I planned to cross over into Canada. I'd heard there was a group in Montreal involved in taking in draft dodgers like myself. Deserters too, of course. I got to Enosburg at eleven o'clock at night on a Tuesday. I hardly had any money left, of course. You know how small Enosburg is, you can't walk down the street at night there without being noticed. I went downtown to get a cup of coffee. And that's where I met the smartest black man I've ever seen."

We turned to Sammy, Françoise and I. He looked at us and he laughed.

"For sure, Ma'am," he said. "You've got to be pretty smart to get out of trouble when you're black and you've run away from the Army. For sure! It's not like those students with their diplomas who have a conscience attack and decide not to wait to be called up and run away nice and quiet like tourists. For sure, Ma'am, draft dodgers have got the easy part, I can tell you that. But us deserters, and black on top of it, we've got everybody after us. For sure!"

But I put my hand on Sammy's arm to stop him talking.

When he starts there's no stopping him, and that's why I came to my sister's place: to talk.

I said to Sammy, "Sure, sure, everybody knows that! And anyway it's not even true. Draft dodger or deserter, when you have the FBI or the MPs after you, you can forget about diplomas and conscience. You're talking about two men, both running. Two men condemned from the start."

I turned to Françoise.

"Let me tell you! You can't imagine what it's like. In Montreal I had a good job, I'd almost made foreman in a steel yard, I had a wife of my own, a little apartment on Clark Street, just below Sherbrooke, my wife had a little girl, then goddamn son of a bitch! I was stupid enough to get caught in a demonstration in front of the American consulate!"

"Can you tell me what you were doing there?"

"I don't even know myself. You're picked up, it's the guys who helped you when you first came who are organizing it, everybody's going, there's nothing to it, you sit down in the street and stay there as long as you can before the police move you on. Only those bastards came in swinging, you had to defend yourself, there were about fifteen of us arrested and obviously I was one of them! There I was, at the station, an American citizen, my three-month visa had expired. The draft dodgers' lawyer came to take care of it and I was released. Then we had a little caucus at the office. It was in the middle of the night. The guys told me there was only one solution: return illegally to the States so I could cross the border back to Canada nice and quiet like a tourist, then once I got back to Montreal, make my official application to Immigration. I never wanted to get involved in that business, immigration formalities and all that crap, but I was caught. I was lucky enough to be free on bail. I couldn't push my luck!"

I turned again to Sammy who was starting to yawn. His eyes were glazed.

"And talk about luck, there he was, right next to me. Sammy said, If you want, man, we'll go across together. I've been wanting to breathe that United States air for a long time.

10

You know what I mean, man? Not the air from *all* the States, not the *official* air of the States, no way! What I want to breathe is the scent of the old South Carolina oaks. Understand, man, I miss the tall pines where they've got the black man's shacks down in South Carolina. If you want we'll go across together. I'm going down to Carolina, you can go back to that Canadian snow if you want to. When I heard that I said, That cat's crazy. He's a deserter! If he gets himself caught it's five years for sure in the brig! I knew I wasn't risking more than three. I'd heard about the amnesty coming up. Not Ford's. Better than that: Mr. Peanut's amnesty! I said to myself, What the hell, I'm going home! And that's how I'm here."

Françoise wanted to serve us more coffee but we noticed that Sammy was already asleep at the end of the table, his head on his arm. We made a place for him on the couch in the living room with a blanket and an embroidered pillow under his head. Sammy was out like a light but we didn't talk too loud anyway. We were standing in the kitchen, facing each other, me and Françoise who had a good grip on her housecoat. She asked, "What are you going to do now?"

"I don't know. I really don't know."

"And your wife and daughter?"

"In Montreal, both of them. I feel like I've just lost them!"

Françoise looked me in the eye a moment then she said, "The same thing is happening to you that happened to your uncle Nazaire."

Nazaire! Of course I'd thought about him during the five years I'd been running and hiding. Exiled in Canada, me, the grandson of a French Canadian who'd immigrated to the States. Hiding in Montreal, hiding like Nazaire. Me too, hiding to keep out of the Army.

We sat down again around the table, Françoise and I. She poured us some coffee and we talked about all that for the rest of the night. Until it got light and the sun began to rise behind the Bradleys' tall pine. We talked about Nazaire. About the time when I was fourteen years old...

11

PART ONE

It was around five o'clock. I remember because the sun was still high on our mountains. Five o'clock or maybe six, time passes quickly and you don't realize it. In any case not later than six, we hadn't had supper yet. It was Willy who noticed it first.

"Nazaire's disappeared. I looked for him everywhere. Didn't find him."

At the beginning we didn't get too worried because there were a lot of people. We told ourselves that Nazaire couldn't have gone too far. Still it was the first time, he never used to wander away. Except into himself, that's for sure. That man Nazaire, he was never completely all there, we never knew if he was really with us. It must have been because of his age. Old people are always detached even if sometimes they pretend not to be, just to be obliging.

Nazaire was between seventy and seventy-five years old. Very short, sturdy and stout, with close-cropped white hair. And most of all his mustache, you would have picked him out of a crowd because of his narrow, bushy mustache, bigger than Hitler's and white too, like his hair. He was my father's brother.

It was in July at my sister Rita's place, along Guillaume's Road, near Lowell, in Vermont, in the little valley that opens out after the clump of pines at the Bradleys', in the middle of our green mountains that aren't real mountains, so they say, but high hills. Not like the Rockies, anyway. But we do have Jay Peak, pointed like the real mountains you see on calendars.

There were a good hundred of us on the grass. The house is big and tall with a covered veranda running all the way around, and at one corner a screened-in porch to keep out the sun, rain and mosquitoes. Like all the houses around here, it's white, made of wood, with a sloping metal roof. When the sun hits it, it makes a light you can see all the way from the mountain. My father gave it to my sister when she got married.

It was a big celebration. We were celebrating my sister's oldest son who'd just graduated eighth grade. There were people everywhere, in the house, on the porch and on the grass. My brother Germain, who plays the accordion, was sitting on a picnic table with cousin Will who'd brought his guitar. They'd been singing since morning. All the country and western tunes that are so pretty to listen to when you're looking off down the valley. You would have thought you were at the Grand Ole Opry in Nashville.

We'd been eating on and off all day. There were three barbecues that had been going non-stop. It smelled like charcoal, grilled meat, sausages and onions. Us kids could have as many hot dogs as we wanted, smothered in mustard and relish, with bottles of Coke, Pepsi and Cream Soda. Bags of potato chips and cupcakes for dessert.

Like at every family reunion, some people played horseshoes. Several of us were watching them, especially because of Paul. It was the first time Paul had played horseshoes since his operation. We said "operation" to not pronounce the word "amputation." He'd had his leg cut off because a tree had fallen on him. His leg had been crushed and he'd yelled until his hired man came to help him. My brother Paul had been happy-go-lucky, always playing tricks. Since his accident, he was a broken man.

That day we'd watched him play horseshoes all afternoon, trying to look as if we weren't observing him too much, to keep from embarrassing him. He was just as good as before. My brother Paul always won. He was the oldest, the one my father

13

had turned over his business to. He was in charge of my father's land, he'd bought up the neighbouring farms, he dealt in hay, he also sold the tanks the farmers buy to store their milk in. He was a man who was sure of himself, a very big man, and he had a mechanical leg.

And then what had to happen happened. Germain, who can't do anything but play tricks when he's not playing his accordion, started to stir up everybody. He bothered the kids. He pulled my sister's daughters' braids and put melon rinds down the boys' backs. As usual it ended up with water, three drops of water on your fingertips, then a wet napkin, then a full glass of water. In the end they were throwing pails of water at each other.

They were playing the worst tricks on each other and laughing. The men had been drinking all afternoon out in the sun. There were cans of Schlitz and Old Milwaukee everywhere. In the end there wasn't any difference between the grown-ups and the kids.

Germain threw a glass of water at Paul's back, and Paul turned around quickly. Germain took off running and Paul watched him go because he couldn't chase him, of course, with his mechanical leg. We pretended to go on being interested in the game and went and sat down as if nothing had happened.

The men, my uncles, some of my brothers and the guests, along with my sister Rita, who always gets involved in the men's conversations, were already on the porch with my father. They were talking politics, in French and in English. Mostly in English because some of them didn't understand French.

At every family reunion they talk politics. This time the conversation was even more lively because we had some cousins from Montreal with us, and also a couple of their friends, people from Nicolet. A little bearded man with glasses and his wife who had great big eyes. People from Canada.

"Goddamn," my father was saying, "do you think, *Monsieur*, that I should regret coming to live here? When everybody was starving to death in Canada?"

The little man said, "yes, but" and my father continued.

"Do you think so? Canada hasn't been back on its feet very many years now. I know, before the Depression I started to do business in Canada. We travelled all over the countryside. It was poor, *Monsieur*, a real shame!"

My father always gets carried away when he talks about the Depression. He took out his handkerchief and wiped his forehead and the corners of his mouth. It's always like that.

"We saw the Depression coming, *Monsieur*. It was hard for everybody but we got over it pretty quickly here in the States. The Canadians have just come out of it. They pulled themselves from poverty, *Monsieur*, not more than ten years ago."

The little man said, "yes, but." His wife was listening wide-eyed.

"Goddamn," my father insisted, "do you think I should be sorry? Especially when you think about what's coming up! When war breaks out, I'd still rather be in the States than in Canada. The United States is the last country that will fall. When the States fall, *Monsieur*, Canada will have disappeared from the map a long time ago."

And my father beat his fist into his hand. The little man said, "But there won't be a war, will there?"

My father was delighted. He prophesied, "We'll have a war before too long, *Monsieur*. Don't you see that money isn't worth a thing any more? First we're going to have a Depression like the last time, then we'll need a war to get back on our feet. It's sad to say but after a Depression you have to have a war to get out of it."

It was July, in the fine six o'clock sunlight. I looked around at the reflection of the roofs of the houses in the valley and I couldn't imagine for an instant that the war could reach us here, in our green mountains, just a few farmers, not poor but not rich enough either to bring a war. New York maybe, but not here.

It was Willy who noticed it first. He whispered in my ear, "Nazaire's disappeared. I looked for him everywhere. Didn't find him."

Among ourselves we called him Nazaire. We said "uncle" to him, of course.

After supper the darkness subdued us. We were in shadow at the bottom of the valley but the summits were still crowned with light. Paul, François, Germain, Rita and the people from Canada had gone in search of Nazaire. They had taken the two tractors and the truck. We heard the sound of the motors fading away little by little in the darkness.

The women were finishing the dishes; there were a lot of them. At noon, since we were outside, those who needed them had taken paper plates and plastic knives and forks, but when we'd gone inside for supper, the news of Nazaire's disappearance made us forget these precautions. We'd eaten in little groups stationed pretty well everywhere, in the living room, on the steps of the staircase and all around the table.

My father, who had hardly eaten, was sitting in the rocker in the kitchen, blowing cigarette smoke toward the big white fluorescent lights on the ceiling. He was still in his Sunday best and he looked preoccupied like he does when he's waiting for somebody in his business.

"Goddamn," he said, "it's my fault, I should have never talked politics! Especially not about the war! But I wasn't paying attention. You can't always be paying attention when you're just family and you're talking just to talk!"

And he beat his fist into his open hand. We were in front of the television set watching the show *What's My Line?* There are four guests who make up a panel. Three characters are led out before them. All three have the same name. The host says, Here's Mr. Jones, he's a shoemaker. Other times he's an aeronautics specialist. All the trades are represented. And the panelists ask questions one at a time to determine which of the three is the real Mr. Jones. When the time is up, the host says, Will the real Mr. Jones please stand up? For a moment all three act as if they're going to stand up but only the real Mr. Jones rises in the end.

And I wasn't the only one, I'm sure, to mingle Nazaire's image with this show. Three Nazaires: which is the real one? Will the real Nazaire please stand up?

"Goddamn," my father grumbled, "shut up, will you? You

can't hear yourself think!"

And he beat his open hand with his fist. My aunt Émilie was already talking about Nazaire in the past tense. Willy asked if there were bears on the mountain. My father was still talking to himself.

"I know he's not quite in his right mind, but he's not crazy either. He'll get along, no problem there. He can sleep in the Bradleys' shed on the third lot. If he goes further there's always the hunting cabin the little Nicholsons built."

One ear on the television and the other on my father, I imagined Nazaire lost in the mountain forests in the company of a certain Mr. Jones, fighting the darkness and the bears. My father was repeating, "It's my fault, I shouldn't have talked about the war."

When the dishes were done, my mother, the aunts and my sisters came to sit down too. Then the men went to walk outside. In front of the house, right in the centre of the lawn, there's a very tall wooden pole, like a mast. Right at the top is the American flag that we bring down every night, of course. And a very powerful light that lights the house, part of the stable and up to the road. That's the Sentinel. The men started to walk in circles on the lawn, hands in their pockets. Some of them took a few steps down the road.

Uncle Eugène cried, "Nazaire, Nazaire!"

But my father got angry and made him quiet down. It was frightening to hear your voice fade away in the night. Then the truck came back.

"I went as far as Lowell," Paul said, "but nobody saw him."

"I knew he hadn't gone that way," my father answered. "He's on the mountain. They'll find him with the tractors."

Then he sat down on the steps and started to think it over. We went inside and got comfortable in front of the television. It must have been between ten and eleven o'clock when we heard the tractors arriving. They were coming back by the cowpath behind the stable. We knew when we saw them that they hadn't found anything. My mother and my aunts started saying we

17

should call the police. My father, who heard everything through the screen door, got angry. He shouted that the police wouldn't do any better than his own boys, that they didn't know the mountain better than they did and that in any case, they were organizing a search-party in the morning and if the police wanted to participate in it, they could.

Alain, my cousin Gilberte's son, did his best to convince Rex, the farm dog, to set off on Nazaire's trail. The animal conscientiously sniffed my uncle's jacket, then went to lie down in one corner of the kitchen. And the evening passed. Around midnight the women remembered they had to put the children to bed. As I was going up I heard my father saying, "He's not crazy but he's not quite in his right mind either. Who knows what a man like him can do? Maybe burn down the forest trying to light a campfire. And there are cliffs by Charlie's place. Anyway, he's crazy enough at his age to poison himself eating bad plants or mushrooms. But the bears are far away this time of year."

Then each of us went upstairs to go to bed. In the morning we woke up, ashamed of having slept.

We live in a country of valleys. That's Vermont. In French that means that our mountains are green, which isn't true all year, of course, since in winter it's all white here, from the summits of the mountains to the slopes of our fields. I was born here and one of my earliest memories, I recall, was that the mountains surrounded our house. That made me think of grown-ups standing over a cradle.

Yet these mountains, or high hills, level out to form the valleys where our houses are scattered. The road disappears in curves and little valleys. It's made of gravel most often; you could follow its route by the wake of dust that rises into the air after the cars go by. You're taken from one farm to the other, and it's always comforting to spot the metal roofs of the barns and houses shining in the sun.

And everything is made of wood here, the mountains and houses alike. The earth itself is made of scraps of wood, dead

18

leaves, bark and rotten trunks that the water has carried into our valleys. But this earth suffers from a sickness: rock. Behind my sister's house the meadow climbs steeply, then right away you reach a plateau that stretches as far as the eye can see toward the distant forest. Rock is king on the plateau.

It's like an ordeal, I really don't know why. I don't know why we deserved this punishment. Maybe it's because most of those who settled here are Canadians. French Canadians on top of it. There are French Canadians everywhere here. There are some in all the New England states.

At school they teach us that we're all Americans. We salute the flag every morning and every evening. But I know that before, I was Canadian and French. My father was born in Canada, my grandfather too. When he was young and lived in Canada, my father spoke only French. In Canada, in his village in the province of Quebec, he didn't speak English. Neither at home nor for his business. Everything was always in French. That's why I'm a little Canadian and French too, even if I became American after all.

My father came here before the Depression. There weren't any other Canadians here. It's the Depression that brought the other ones here. They were starving to death in Canada. So they came here to work in the textile mills.

Of course these French Canadians settled where the other French Canadians were. Then the priests arrived so the French Canadians would stay Catholic and go on talking French. That's how villages formed around the little white wooden churches. French-Canadian villages. Today there are almost as many Canadians as real Americans around here.

But there's no difference. We're like everybody else. We talk American at school and in the stores. American everywhere. Only sometimes at home in the evening our parents talk a little French to us, to keep us from forgetting. Forgetting what?

When we woke up we couldn't even see Jay Peak. You could have cut the fog with a knife. It must have been seven o'clock.

19

My father, Paul and Germain were already in the kitchen. Willy and I went downstairs, still putting on our clothes. We felt as if we were late to an important ceremony. My father had already called the sheriff in Troy, we'd heard him as we were dressing.

Frank O'Connor is the sheriff, a fat man who eats and sleeps a lot. He was just re-elected. He was sleeping when my father called him on the phone to announce Nazaire's disappearance. At first the fat man didn't seem to understand why somebody would disturb him for that so early in the morning. Then my father got angry, he reminded him that his brother was seventy-five years old and he'd had to explain that the old man wasn't quite in his right mind. My brothers pretended not to listen as they drank their coffee.

Then the women got up, my mother, my sisters, we were all in the kitchen, the cousins from Canada and their friends, when the phone rang. It was O'Connor calling back to announce he would personally go to see the priest and the minister of the three Protestant churches to ask them to summon the population to participate in a search-party. Fortunately it was Sunday, the people of Troy and Lowell would all be informed.

The sheriff had hesitated about whether he should ask the volunteers to go off in small groups, or whether he shouldn't bring them all instead to my sister's house after church was over. He finally decided to rally all his people together because, so he'd said, fifty men would be more efficient in the woods and on the mountain than little groups of ten or even twenty. The meeting was set for eleven o'clock.

We sat down to breakfast in silence. A big Sunday breakfast, with eggs, bacon and little fried potatoes. It must have been around nine o'clock now. The fog was clinging to the summits of the mountains but you could see the earth below like a sleeper's unmade bed. Nazaire must have lain down there, somewhere in the woods. It hadn't been cold enough to endanger even a man of his age. Not for just one night, in any case. But the night is still the night!

My father's ancestors lived in Nicolet in the province of Quebec.

The first one to come to that town was François, a big tall man from l'Islet, a sailor who'd also built schooners, for himself and for other people. He was a man with a sure hand, who could boast he'd never made a false cut with his plane. We never knew why he'd left l'Islet. He came to the province of Quebec just like that, with his courage and his two big hands.

In those days Quebec was poor, even poorer than today. It was all farmers. They ate their fill but they worked from sun-up to sun-down. In the towns there were priests, notaries and lawyers, most of all lawyers because the French Canadians were always suing each other. A few doctors too, for the men and for the animals. Those who weren't farmers or lawyers worked for the lawyers. They painted their houses, repaired their furniture, weeded their gardens and trimmed their apple trees. A good little orderly life, not very rich but nobody was unhappy. They didn't know anything better.

Our ancestor François offered his services to the lawyers too. In the end the lawyers were working for him. When two farmers were having a quarrel they went to see the lawyer. He made them settle and took their money. Then the lawyer needed to have the porch of his house repaired. François did the work, the lawyer gave him some money, but François, he didn't give that money back to anybody. He kept it for himself. François didn't need anybody else.

He was a generous man, he had sixteen children. And to feed all those children he slaved away so hard that in the end he found himself at the head of a little carpentry and cabinet-making business. He bought woodlots, he chopped down trees all winter in snow up to his belly, he got the old Seigneurie Trigge's sawmill running again, he cut up his trees, he did everything himself. He built houses, and he even went as far as building a convent. Doors, windows, furniture too, and some-times even coffins when it was necessary.

Almost everybody in my family worked in the business, from father down to son. François left it to his oldest, Eugène, who had himself given it to Louis, my grandfather. And that way my father and my uncles just naturally found their place in the business, too. A fine path, drawn out straight before them. Only one man refused to fall into step: Nazaire.

By ten o'clock some volunteers had already arrived. We were outside, in the yard and on the lawn, like the night before. We were waiting for everybody to be there before we left.

We were in two camps, us and the others, and at times some of ours would go over to the others to explain the business to them and tell them all the particulars. In the end I'd heard the same explanations a good ten times.

My father was standing in the middle of the yard in his Sunday best, his hands in his pockets, and he was talking with the newcomers. Paul, Germain, François and I were next to him—and Rita too, who's always with the men.

"Goddamn," my father was saying, "it's my fault. It happened yesterday. We were all there, it was a big family get-together, we were celebrating my sister's oldest boy's graduation. There we were on the porch, talking just for the hell of it, about politics, the Depression and the war. Goddamn, I should have kept quiet! It's all my fault. I wasn't paying attention to him. I hadn't noticed him. He's been part of the family since he came here to end his days with us. You know what an old man's like."

"Yeah," said the people from Troy and Lowell.

"You know what it's like," my father went on, "an old man closed up in himself who's afraid of everything. Afraid of women, afraid of kids, afraid of himself. Afraid of life, you might say. Afraid that the life in him will be too strong and that he'll die of it. Think of what it's like: a scared old man right in the middle of a family get-together. You laugh, you talk loud, you do and say crazy things. So the scared old man sticks to the oldest ones because he thinks he's like them. He sits down next to them and he listens. He hears them talking politics, especially about the Depression, about the one we had and about the one that's coming. He hears them talking about the war too. They're saying that if things keep on, there's going to be a war, it's inevitable. And he feels more and more alone. He knows he's not on the side of the women, he knows he's not on the side of the children, he knows he's not on the side of the other old men. He knows he's all alone. So he disappears. Where to? Nobody knows. What for? Nobody knows that either. He's running away from the war as though it were about to break out any minute."

"Poor man," said the people from Troy and Lowell.

And I was watching them, the people from Troy and Lowell, and I didn't know what to think. I did know they had to be there to help us find Nazaire. I knew that but I couldn't get used to them being there. I couldn't even keep myself from hating them a little, because of their indifference. They weren't there to help us find Nazaire: they'd come out of curiosity. I said to myself, it's the crowd, the one that always gathers when there's been an accident. The crowd that lives off the misfortunes of others.

I know, I've seen it before. I was very young then. My father had bought some land by Eden Mills. It was poor and up in the hills. My father buys everything, even if it's on the poor side. He buys fallow land, he hires a man and the next year the field is yielding a lot. There was a big plot of land full of little valleys with big slabs of rock in some places and especially scrub, everywhere, little wild trees that eat the earth, like my father says. The first time we went to inspect the place, I heard the monstrous little trees with their thousands of crooked roots eating the earth. It gave me the creeps to walk on it. I was right too, because a month later, when we went back there with the farmer my father had just hired, a terrible thing had happened.

We knew right away something had happened. They were all there, the same ones, far off in the fields, looking at the ground. We came closer, my father called to me to wait, not to run. I didn't hear a thing. I slipped into the middle of the circle. There was a shallow ditch. The earth had been turned over. We saw something like a piece of clothing, a shirt maybe, and a rough orange strip like a pumpkin rind. It was a stomach. It was the skin from the stomach of a man who'd been buried there. He'd been missing for about two weeks. They'd searched for him everywhere. They'd organized search-parties. There must have been a hundred of them in all. They'd searched for several days in a row. Some children found him, some children who were going fishing in the South Pond creek. They were walking in the ditch because there was less scrub there. It was autumn, I remember, the grass was yellow and brown. First the children found a rubber boot. Right away they thought of the man who had disappeared. Then they stepped on something soft, freshly turned earth. They dug with their hands. They unearthed the pumpkin rind and the scrap of clothing. They went off running of course, and told the people in Eden Mills. Then everybody arrived at the same time. Not only men, women too, and a lot of children. The sheriff, of course. They were all there, it's always like that when there's been an accident. They were all there but nobody ever knew who had buried the man in the ditch. They were all there, but that didn't change a thing.

My father talked to me a lot about Nicolet, about this little town crowned with steeples, with its wooden sidewalks and houses pressed one against the other, turning their backs to the river. It really was a small town, five thousand inhabitants, more or less as it is today. People from another age, no happier or unhappier than those of today.

At one time there were four music shops in Nicolet. In other words, those people must not have been unhappy all the time. They rose at five o'clock in the morning in winter, it's true, to walk through the blizzard to church. But they must have laughed too, at times, when they played their instruments. They must have played to chase away the thought that they would have to get up the next day at five o'clock. They let their fiddles say what they themselves would never have dared express out loud.

You see them on an engraving that my father kept, you see them in the low kitchen of an old-fashioned house, the table pushed against the stove, their arms around the local girls, dancing the jig under the amused eye of the old men and the musicians. The priest is there, looking on with a disapproving countenance. But he's powerless as long as the musicians let their instruments speak. That's why when the tune was finished, my father recalls, the dancers cried *"Encore!"* all together. And the musicians didn't have to be asked twice. The combat could last for nights on end. There were the priests, the musicians, the fathers, mothers and children, more or less like today. Neither more unhappy nor less happy than today.

Still, it seems Nazaire wasn't a child like the rest. Already he worried his parents when he was a little boy. It's difficult for me to imagine Nazaire as a child. People who didn't have cars or trucks, who'd never seen an airplane. Who didn't leave their houses all winter. People from Canada.

So to understand better, I put myself in his shoes. Fairly tall, blonde, with a few freckles. I had to change clothes, put on a bigger pair of pants and shirt, barefoot, with a big straw hat. I walked down a dirt track bordered by twisted willows, a fishing rod over my shoulder, made from a thin branch and rough twine rolled up at one end with a mean-looking hook. A picture from an old calendar.

That's how I imagine Nazaire as a child. To understand him better still, I could take on his feelings, but they say he was sad. They said Nazaire searched for happiness all his life like a dog chasing its tail. I wasn't sad—well, not too sad. So I tried to recall the times I had been and I said to myself that it must have always been like that for him.

He was like that from his earliest childhood. All alone in a corner, rocking on his wooden horse. Later, when the others were playing cowboys and Indians, he stayed sitting for hours, digging holes in the sand. In winter, standing on a snowdrift, watching darkness fall.

I suppose he must have gotten used to his sadness a little. He must have simply become melancholy instead. A melancholy that makes for silence. That's why people thought he was sad. People were poor in those days but that wasn't any reason to be sad. I know that children had to walk through the Canadian snow to go to school, but everybody did it and all the children weren't sad. His own sadness must have been in him from birth, like a weakness or a disease. Sometimes there are children born with a frail constitution. Nazaire must have been born sad.

That's why he was always alone. Children his age weren't interested in him. He went fishing on his own. He went to school on his own. Sometimes he didn't even go to school. Nobody knew where he went; he never said. He was punished, of course, his father would unbuckle his leather belt but Nazaire didn't say a word. He would stay kneeling in the corner without his supper rather than promise not to do it again. In the end his mother took pity on him. She used to say he was a difficult child. When all the others were asleep she gave him a piece of bread before sending him up to bed too.

Once, I don't know how old he was, he disappeared for four days. He was around fourteen, my age now. Already he'd stopped going to school. He didn't want to go to school any more, they'd done everything to force him, it was useless. His parents had finally given in. He wasn't working either. He must have just been sad.

It was summer. Summer in Canada is like it is here, warm with mosquitoes everywhere. It's like here but there are no mountains. Not in Nicolet, in any case. It's all flat.

Nazaire had disappeared. They thought he'd drowned fishing. People dragged the river bottom with big hooks. They found nothing but tree stumps. Others organized search-parties in the marshes along Lake Saint-Pierre. There are little willows and water weeds there as tall as a man. They used to say that anybody who lost his way in there might have a chance of survival, but that he'd never get out on his own.

But Nazaire found his way out all by himself. He simply came back to the house four days later, at suppertime. They never found out anything—he didn't say a word. He wasn't even punished. His parents knew it was useless. But he must have had his reasons. I would have had mine.

There were a lot of people in the yard at my sister's place, people from Troy and Lowell. They were talking about Nazaire even if they didn't know him. Nazaire arrived here no more than six months ago. He never wanted to come before.

My father always said it had taken him fifteen years to convince his brother to come live here with us in the States. Nazaire was all by himself in his house in Nicolet, in the province of Quebec, in Canada. They said he'd shut himself up there after the death of his wife. My father said that Nazaire was like a wounded animal.

He was like me, the way I felt when I'd built myself the treehouse at the top of the meadow. It's simple. Sometimes you want to, other times you need to. I'd spend ten minutes or two hours there. It's all the same. You don't feel the time passing when you're busy letting yourself float in the clouds. The clouds in your head, I mean. We were of the same race, Nazaire and I. The race of dreamers.

And he had a trade that makes you sad, Nazaire did. He was a blacksmith. He lived on the rue Mélançon, the smallest street in the town of Nicolet. It was near the station, a street so small you would have taken it for the entrance to the hotel courtyard. A street of about thirty houses, a world firmly set apart where nobody even went.

It was a fairly large wooden house, painted green. Since his wife died, Nazaire hadn't looked after the maintenance. The storm windows were never washed or even taken down in the summer. In the winter, the screen doors slammed in the wind. The balcony and the veranda had swelled like the belly of an old person. The paint was scaly like the skin of old men.

My father told me about the kitchen that occupied almost all the first floor, like in the old-fashioned houses. A kitchen for big families, ten, twelve children, plus visitors, plus the beggar. Room for everybody. A kitchen made for the smell of soup, for laughter and shouts. A big two-tiered, chrome wood stove, with, say, three or four rockers around it and the beggar's bench near the door. Nazaire had lived alone in that kitchen these last fifteen years.

In the winter, he tended the fire. That's how it was in the

27

old days, and that's the way Nazaire remained. He spent all winter by the stove, day and night, dozing off in his chair. Poking the fire from time to time, putting on a piece of wood, emptying the ashes. Shaking out his pipe on the ash-guard of the stove. They both produced ashes, Nazaire and the stove. Day and night, all winter.

In the summer too, he found a way to spend a good deal of his time in that kitchen. He slept on a couch set against the wall behind the table. He said the kitchen was the coolest room in the house.

My father said he didn't remember the rooms upstairs. He'd slept there sometimes when he was visiting, but after Nazaire's wife died, the upstairs had been closed off and nobody went up there any more. Fifteen years.

All because Nazaire had a trade that makes you sad. He was a blacksmith. The yard behind his house was closed in by sheds. He had his forge in the one at the back, a forge like in the old days, black, dark, with a fire at the very bottom and a big pedal bellows. A gigantic anvil too.

In the summer, he was there when six o'clock struck and he managed to keep himself busy until the sun went down. With, in spite of his schedule, time for a nice nap in the afternoon. In the winter, especially toward the end, he gave up going there completely. He said he couldn't leave the fire alone in the kitchen, that it was too dangerous.

Nazaire was a blacksmith, but it had been a long time since he'd worked his forge. The time of the blacksmiths was long over. Instead he repaired tools, bent, twisted, soldered, sometimes even straightened an automobile chassis. A jack-of-all-trades.

Nazaire had a trade that makes you sad. And when he wasn't working, he still managed to busy himself with his hands. He whittled. Anything, bits of wood, twigs, even peach pits. He made tops and little baskets out of peach pits. All alone. For himself. For nothing.

He worried people. They did their best to convince him not to live alone. My father wrote to the sisters of Precious Blood

28

whose convent was near his house. He asked them to send the chaplain to see his brother as often as possible. He wrote to a lady named Parenteau who had been connected, I don't know in what way, to my grandfather's family. He asked her to go to Nazaire's house to see to his domestic upkeep and he sent her money in return. Nazaire greeted everybody politely but he cut the conversations short. Once he'd even fallen asleep, so they say, while the Precious Blood chaplain was visiting. In the end they agreed that Nazaire might be a little feeble-minded. But that didn't make them any less worried.

My father made a special trip to Nicolet to try to settle the question once and for all. He threatened to put Nazaire in an old folks' home. The old man laughed in his face. My father came back furious, saying he'd done his duty and that he didn't want to hear anything more about that old fool. But the next day he wrote once more to Precious Blood and the lady named Parenteau.

Then Nazaire finally came to live with us. I don't know what had persuaded him. One evening when he came back home, my father announced that Uncle would be coming to live with us. That was all. Two weeks later, Nazaire was there, sitting in the kitchen rocking chair, not saying a word.

At first we thought he was keeping quiet because he didn't understand American. We began speaking French to him but he didn't answer. He smoked his pipe, that was all. Stubbornly, he kept quiet. One day, however, he said to me with a half-smile, "Here, my boy, take this."

He held out a pocket knife, an old one with a worn handle, and two little tops carved out of peach pits.

"Try and do the same."

I wondered what they were waiting for. The sheriff, my father and the men didn't agree, I guess, about what steps to take. They tried to imagine where Nazaire could have gone. They tried to put themselves in his shoes. "Take an old man," they said, "who's afraid and who runs away to hide. He doesn't need to go very far. First thing he does is disappear into the woods and he starts to feel safe. But let's say he wants to get away a little farther to be good and sure he won't be found. He walks straight ahead. He crosses the fields where the hay is tall. He goes into the woodlots. He crosses two or three clearings, then he thinks he's reached the end of the world. He stops, especially since he's old and tired, and from there on it starts to climb steeply. He tells himself if ever he hears voices, if he realizes someone is searching for him, he'd only have to make one last effort to disappear for good among the rocks and pine trees that rise up in front of him."

"It's not so simple," my father said. "You don't know him."

And he fell silent as if he was afraid of letting something out. The sheriff was starting to get impatient. He wanted to leave right away. He'd been trying to form the groups for the last fifteen minutes.

"Cy, Walter, Reggie, Bill, your brother too, Lennie, Max, you too, Sam, you go over there. No, not you, Germain, I want you for another group. Listen, men. Each group will scout out straight ahead. I'll send another party down from Black Hill. Listen to me. Listen. Each group..."

He was shouting now.

"Don't hang back! Please, Mister Donohue, please! Order, please! Each group..."

But the men weren't listening. They were busy talking among themselves and forming hypotheses. The sheriff was getting impatient. He went off angrily to his pick-up truck. Some of the men thought he was going to leave but he came back equipped with a battery-powered loud-speaker. Despite his considerable bulk, he managed to hoist himself up on the hood of Fred Dennisson's car. We knew his rough shoes must be scratching the paint. We stopped talking and looked up at him.

From above the sheriff overlooked all of the yard and part of the road. There were cars everywhere, trucks too, and a few tractors. There were even vehicles parked on the steep slope across from the house. Fifty men in a circle in the yard who were quiet now. The women all together on the porch and the lawn.

"Okay, men!" the sheriff shouted into the loudspeaker. "Okay! It's time now! No more fun, it's time to work. The old man has been in the hills all night long. Those who do not intend to be serious may leave. We need no shirkers and no fooling around. You, the first group, start down the road. Stay there, stay, hey, I mean stay on the road! Now the second group will rally by the stables. You, from there to there, you too, not you, you!"

While the sheriff was shouting, my father went from one group to the next. His will was beginning to shape the gathering. Now there were two groups, one on the road and another near the stables. He divided the remainder of the men into two other camps. My father, Paul, Germain and us kids were standing around the sheriff, near Fred Dennisson's car, a new Impala.

"I don't want any kids in the search," the sheriff said, glaring at us. "Listen, everybody! You on the road, you take the trucks and go to Bill's place, I mean Bill Price. Go up on the mountain as high as you can with the vehicles. Then come back down here and search every bush. You take your gun with you, Lennie. If you find him, fire one shot. The second group will patrol the area of the peak. The others will follow me."

And turning toward my father, he said, "We have to find him. Missing the baseball game on TV is bad enough. I know it's only the Indians and the White Sox, but I wanted to watch it like everybody else."

"Ten bucks on the *Indiens*," Reggie announced.

The men around burst out laughing. The sheriff picked up his loud-speaker again and his harsh voice rose with it.

"Okay, now! We break at six o'clock. Get back here for report."

Then the groups got moving. Trucks and cars pulled away on the road. An old GMC pick-up sitting crosswise that they couldn't get started. Groups of children practically pushing each other under the wheels. Bicycles abandoned on the edge of the ditch. Women running to give supplies to their men. Shouts and calls from one group to the other.

31

The sheriff was doing his best to convince Paul to give up the idea of coming with us.

"You'll get tired," he said, "and you'll hold us up. Try to understand!"

"I could keep up with you the whole day," Paul protested.

"Paul, you stay here!" my father cut in.

And I was getting ready to slip in discreetly behind them. The sheriff had said "no kids" but I wasn't a kid any more. I had Nazaire's knife in my pocket.

The yard emptied. The women were still outside watching the dust thin out along the road. It was a little after twelve and the sun was beating down hard. Deep inside, I had a thought I was a little ashamed of. I was hoping they wouldn't find Nazaire too quickly, to make the fun last.

Fifty men were fanning out across the mountain side in search of Nazaire. Fifty men to find one poor old man who wanted to be alone at any cost. I followed the sheriff and my father's group, a few steps away, far enough not to be noticed but still close enough to hear the conversations. What I heard was still foreign to me back then. Perhaps I was too far back in childhood. I was going to have to lose my wife and daughter and no longer feel at home in my own country to understand what my memories meant.

"Goddamn," my father was saying, "you've got to be crazy! Just look at us! A fine Sunday in July! We should be playing horseshoes and drinking beer! Or filling the pick-up full of kids and going to play a ball game against the Lowell altar-boys. Or else putting the television out on the lawn, in the shade, and just watching the Indians play the white Sox. Instead of that, we're sweating blood climbing up the mountain. With the flies and the mosquitoes!"

It seemed to me that my father's anger grew as he talked. It

32

was as if his anger was fed by his words.

"He's just an old man," Fred Dennisson said.

"He may be old," my father replied, "but I'm telling you he's nuts. Even when he was a little boy he never did anything like anybody else. For instance, on Sunday, my father and mother would take us all to high Mass at the cathedral, my brothers, my sisters and me. In our little outfits that our mother had sewn us from the older ones' clothes."

The men laughed in the thick air.

"Father took us to Mass," he went on. "There were nine children, but at the time I'm telling you about, there must have been a couple who were still too small to go to church. There must have been seven of us, and Nazaire was there too. In those days in the churches, we had assigned seats we rented and that we were proud of. Our family's pew was one of the first ones in front. We never got there late, but just before the service began. It was important to let everybody see us. All the more important because our church was a cathedral, and being near the choir showed how important we were in the town. My father, and my grandfather too, I think, had worked on the construction of the cathedral. We walked the length of the nave down the main aisle, my father and my mother in front and the children behind, every which way but quiet and respectful. All except Nazaire who, once again, wasn't with the others. Nazaire belonged to the choir. This honour redeemed him in my parents' eyes. They were very proud to know that their little boy had been chosen as one of the thirty most beautiful voices in Nicolet to sing the praises of the Lord. And all week, every time Nazaire got into trouble, they consoled themselves with the thought that the following Sunday the Saviour would forgive him everything, as they themselves did when they heard how pure he sang. Then one day my father could hold out no longer. More than anything else he wanted to see his child who he imagined high above in the angels' choir. Coming back from communion, he went past his pew and walked to the back of the church. Quickly he climbed the creaking stairs that led to the organ loft. The entire

33

cathedral was vibrating at that solemn moment. My father stopped just at the top of the stairs and, without being seen, began inspecting the thirty children rendering homage to the Saviour at the very moment of His descent into the hearts of men. He examined each face, began again, moved forward a little, then finally planted himself squarely in front of the chorus. Brother Michel, the director, was encouraging his boys with one hand as he turned to my father and gave him a questioning look. 'Where is my son?' asked my father. 'What son?' he answered. 'Nazaire, of course.' 'But *Monsieur*, he was never part of the choir!' And Brother Michel went back to beating out the measure with his two hands, which revived the choir of his angels. My father climbed down the stairs heavily. He leaned against a column near the portico and peered into the shadows. Once high Mass was over, he was among the first to leave and he posted himself near the doors. Nazaire wasn't long in appearing. 'Where are you coming from?' my father asked him. Astonished, Nazaire stared at him without saying a word. 'Don't bother lying!' my father added. Then Nazaire understood that he had better tell the truth. He ended up admitting that he had never been part of the choir and that he used to attend Mass all alone, off to one side, leaning against a column. And my father never could get an answer to his question, though he asked it a good ten times: 'Why? Are you ashamed to come sit with us in front? Why?' But admitting his lie was already saying enough for Nazaire. He must not have figured he had to justify his actions, since he added nothing more. So you see," my father said, happy with his demonstration, "Nazaire wasn't a child like the rest."

"Some special kind of a kid," the sheriff said.

"Bad enough if they were alone in the world," said my father. "But they're the bane of everybody around them."

Concealed behind the trunk of a big oak, I began to feel like Nazaire when he was a child, hiding behind a pillar in the Nicolet cathedral, listening, my eyes wide.

But at the same time I couldn't help hearing my heart

pounding as if it would leap from my chest. I was learning as much from what came to me from within.

The mountain side rang with cries and laughter and songs. My brother Germain's accordion:

> I come from Alabama
> With my banjo on my knee.
> I'm bound for Louisiana
> My true love for to see.

We reached the plateau at the end of Guillaume's Road; there the land isn't cultivated any more. We began walking on the forest roads and the sun was no more than a play of rays of light through the tree branches, mostly pines, dense and sweet-smelling. The air had a thickness almost like honey. Thousands of flies were buzzing in the underbrush.

Old Cy Bradley was walking ahead of us. His two sons, Walter and Reggie, were keeping to themselves because they didn't like their father's company. They were waiting impatiently for him to die so they could run the family farm, and they didn't mind talking about it, sometimes even in front of the man himself.

My brother François had gathered the Ryan boys, Lennie and Max, around him. The Ryans' hired man, Sam, who didn't naturally join any group, drifted over to them. Bringing up the rear were the sheriff and my father. And me fifty paces further back, from one tree to the next.

The men were deployed as if they were on a hunting party. Almost everybody had brought his rifle and Max had finally released his two beagles. We were really going hunting. We were going to try to flush out an old man.

"It reminds me of the war," the sheriff said. "We'd landed in Normandy, in France. We heard the cannon fire that made the ground tremble under our feet. The damn Germans were all over. We knew we were going to win, we were going to kick their asses, but in the meantime they were everywhere. Hiding everywhere, the lousy bastards! We had to go get them one by one. I'd

35

landed on Omaha Beach with the first reinforced division. A few days later, under the command of General Patton, we were just outside Alençon. We were in the middle of a clean-up operation."

I listened to Sheriff O'Connor, and I gripped Nazaire's knife in my pocket. The fat man was talking like someone who loves war, like a man who's proud of having been in the war. Who even misses the war.

"We had flame-throwers," he said. "You should have seen them come out of their holes! No prisoners. They'd bugged our asses long enough. They'd killed enough of our guys. No quarter, no prisoners. As soon as we saw one come out of his hole, ta ta ta ta ta. They danced like puppets, ta ta ta ta ta."

The sheriff was shouting as if he really was in the war, on the plateau at the end of Guillaume's Road. The others had stopped and they were listening to him and looking at him. The fat man was playing war in the pines of our Vermont forests, in the middle of a July afternoon, a Sunday on top of it all.

He dashed toward a bush, machine gun in his hands.

"Get out of there!" he shouted. "Get out of there, you lousy rats! Ta ta ta ta ta."

He called us to bear witness.

"That was when we got out our flame-thrower," he said.

And Sheriff O'Connor pointed the stream of his flame-thrower toward the lair of the indomitable Jerries.

"Shhhhhhhhhh," he blew to imitate the murderous weapon.

And the indomitable Jerries came out to writhe in flames before our eyes on the carpet of pine needles.

I'd just had the time to jump behind a pine bush when the men stopped and the sheriff's charades led them toward me. I hit the dirt like a German before the thundering advance of General Patton's troups.

"How's it going?" the sheriff shouted into an imaginary telephone. "Situation normal all fucked up," he answered himself in the hurried voice of a hero who has no time to waste on reports.

He grabbed a long, pointed branch.

36

"Some of them had hidden in the hay in the barns," he said. "Then we'd get out the pitchforks."

He jabbed his pointed stick around the spot where I was huddled.

"Get out of there!" he yelled. "Hands up, get out of there, you lousy rats!"

As soon as the imaginary prisoners came out in front of the pine bush, he hurried to machine gun them. I was terrified and I didn't move. I was terrified and angry at the same time. I hated the sheriff and all those men who were his accomplices through silence. Luckily, the sheriff had other enemies to pursue, and he moved further from my spot.

For a long time I was still. I remembered now that Nazaire had run away when he heard my father bring up the Depression and the war. Perhaps he *had* known what war was like, and that memory was unbearable. Today I know what the thought of war can do to a man's heart.

I caught myself wishing hard that the sheriff and his men wouldn't be able to find Nazaire. Because I was afraid for him if ever he fell into their hands.

Nazaire must have been seventeen or eighteen at the time of the First World War, and I had no doubt that he'd fought in it. I knew that neither he nor my father had been in the Second World War, the one just before I was born, but in 1914 they must have been of the age to give their lives for their country. Both of them must have gone off to war and conducted themselves like heroes. It was unquestionable. Men of the caliber of my father and Nazaire had swept the German tide from Europe.

I had to hit the dirt like the enemy. It was getting hotter and hotter. The sun had managed to filter into the underbrush and had thickened the air.

"It reminds me of the war," the sheriff had started saying again.

My father interrupted him.

"Don't talk about the war all the time," he said sharply.

"It's true, you talk about the war all the time! It gets on my nerves! Besides, you know Nazaire ran away yesterday afternoon when he heard us talking about the war."

"Bad memories, maybe," said the sheriff.

"More than you think," my father cut in. "Nazaire fought the war in one strange way, let me tell you. Especially since it wasn't the French Canadians' war!"

The sheriff jumped.

"It was everybody's war!" he shouted. "The first one and the second one too! It was the free world's war! We were fighting for freedom!"

"Maybe we were fighting for freedom, but we didn't have the choice to go or not!"

"That's when we found out the difference between the men and the boys! I wasn't around for the first one," the sheriff went on vehemently, "and I'm sorry I wasn't! In any case, in 1940 I was one of the first to enlist. I was ready to go and fight, I'd have given anything to go and fight. I went, and if I had to do it over again—"

My father interrupted him. "Just listen to yourself! You talk like a man who misses the war!"

"There's no shame!" exclaimed the sheriff. "It was for honour and freedom! I killed plenty of Germans! I fired into the lot of them and I was happy. We didn't always know if our bullets hit their mark but we were out to kill as many as we could. I killed a lot more Germans than I could count."

"In any case," my father cut in, "we didn't go to war, not Nazaire, and not me."

The men halted. They looked at my father, then they came closer to him. Old Cy lit his pipe and sat down on a stump. He wanted to hear more. His two sons and the hired man were there too with my brothers. And I was dug in behind my bush like a German. The sun was holding all Vermont in its hand.

"We didn't go to war," repeated my father. "We didn't feel like fighting their *maudite guerre*."

The sheriff started getting angry.

"You're cowards like all the other French Canadians. Do

you know what would have happened if everybody had done the same as you two? There'd be Germans everywhere around here and we'd have lost everything, our freedom and democracy."

He shot my father a challenging glance: he had just spoken fighting words. The men fell silent, my father too. The sheriff faced him. They were fighting their own war in the heavy silence of the Vermont forest. And my father had become the enemy.

"I didn't go to war," he said slowly, "because I knew there'd be enough men like you who'd want to fight. Us French Canadians didn't have anything to do with it. It was the English, French and German war."

"The Americans won the war," the sheriff said in an offended voice. "We won it!"

"The Americans went to defend England," replied my father. "Us French Canadians didn't have anything to do with it. Not with the English and not with the French. After what they'd done to us!"

"We defended the free world," the sheriff said.

"Us French Canadians," said my father, "we didn't have the time or the means to go defending other people. We had too many things to do in our own country. We were a pretty poor bunch in those days. And we were manufacturing for the war. I worked for the war too. I was in a glasses factory at the time. The glasses we made were for the soldiers. Can you see that, a soldier without his glasses?"

The men began to laugh quietly.

Just then they heard the sound. I heard it too, huddled behind my bush, and better than they did no doubt, but I couldn't show my face. It was just behind my spot, at the top of a steep slope. The vegetation had been torn away by some monstrous force, and you could see the naked belly of the earth, with her rocks and yellow sand.

A distinct sound, footsteps in the underbrush, snapping twigs and the huh! huh! of panting, then the rustling of branches and leaves as if someone had begun moving again.

The men turned around all at the same time toward the spot where the sound had come from. Suddenly they remembered the reason they were here, in the mountain forest. They had talked about a man in the past tense as if he had disappeared forever. Now the mysterious sound was going to put them back on Nazaire's trail. And what if it was Nazaire they'd just heard? He might have spotted us a while ago and had hidden to follow us.

Behind my bush, without knowing why, I was hoping they wouldn't find him right away. Not like that. And I realized I had taken Nazaire's knife from my pocket and peeled all the bark off a live branch of a little maple in arm's reach.

"Listen to me," my father shouted, "listen to me! He can't be very far. We'll call him all together. Everybody turn in the direction you're facing. Na-zaire! Na-zaire!"

The men cupped their hands around their mouths. They turned in every direction. Some shouted toward the forest below, others toward the confines of the plateau, others toward the summit.

"Na-zaire! Na-zaire!"

The other group answered. They rushed down the slope screaming, like Indians on TV.

"Crazy fools," my father muttered.

Bill Price was in front of him, bare-chested, his shirt wrapped around his head to protect him from the sun and all red. He was in front of my father, his legs apart, and he was reeling.

"Your old man's lost," he said. "If he'd been there we would have found him. He's good and lost," he added solemnly, raising his finger like a preacher.

My father sized him up, undisturbed.

"In your state," he answered, "I'm not surprised you didn't find him. If he'd been there, you would have walked right by him."

Bill Price turned to the others who had gathered around him. He called them to witness with grand gestures. They were all in a circle around my father like Indians surrounding a prisoner.

"How do you like that?" said Bill Price. "The guy is upset. We spend our Sundays running up and down the mountain, looking for his old nut, we're hot, we're thirsty, we're sweating blood and he's not happy!"

He pointed at my father, shaking a bottle of Seagram's in his fist. From where I was, it really looked like a scene between the white men and the Indians.

"You're all a bunch of drunk pigs!" my father said.

"Shut up, you!" said Bill Price. "I'm not in the mood to be insulted by some old nut!"

The men were muttering behind his back. Bill Price went on insulting my father.

"We spend our whole Sunday on the mountain finding his old nut and *Monsieur* isn't happy. *Monsieur* thinks we've drunk too much. One more word..."

"Watch out," my father growled.

They were face to face and my father put his hand on Bill Price's shoulder.

"If it wasn't for your grey hair," said Bill Price, "you'd know who you're dealing with! Now get your hand off my shoulder!"

That's when Willy, red as a beet, stuck his fist in Bill Price's face. The sheriff stepped forward to break them up but the Bradley boys had already gone for Bill Donohue.

"Stop it!" shouted the sheriff, running from one group to the other. "Stop it! Bunch of wildcats! No fighting! Stop it!"

But the men were fighting with full force. You heard them grunting like animals. Willy and the hired man jumped on Bill Price and they were hitting him in the head with their fists. Bill Price had a bloody nose. My father was trying to stop the battle.

"*Arrêtez*," he cried. "For the love of God, stop it! This is no time to fight! The old man's lost!"

The sheriff's harsh voice rang out, louder than my father's.

"Stop it! Bunch of wildcats!"

But the men were deaf. They fought without hearing a thing. It was as if fighting did them good. As if it filled a need. They had been drinking, my father was right, but there was

41

more than that. It might have come from the wildness of the landscape. They rarely went up this high and especially never everybody at once. They seemed to take pleasure in fighting.

That's when the sheriff fired his revolver into the air. The men stopped in their tracks. They were already stock-still when the fat man fired the second shot. Then we heard a shot in the distance, down below, toward the west, from the direction the other group must have gone at noon. Judging from the strength of the shot, they must have been beyond Creek River, maybe even further than Long Pond.

The men looked at each other.

"They think we found him!" my father said.

"It's your fault!" the sheriff replied.

"Just bad luck," my father answered.

Bill Price's nose was bleeding. Willy and the hired man were doing their best to stop the blood with their handkerchiefs. They were holding his head back, and his body was propped up by old Cy's coat.

It was like a battlefield. It was as if we'd lost the war. Six o'clock had passed. By the time we climbed down, the sun would be setting on our mountains. Then the sky would turn purple and slowly night would fall.

"There's nothing left to do but turn back," my father said.

The sheriff nodded his approval. Already the men were set to begin their walk down the mountain.

"It won't be too cold tonight," said my father. "We'll come back tomorrow. Maybe he already went home."

"Maybe," said the sheriff. "He might have gone back all by himself."

In silence, we began heading down.

PART TWO

"Poor old man," my father said.

He was straddling his chair, his elbows on the back. He ran his hand through his white hair.

"Poor old man," he repeated. "Being all alone on the mountain is just the beginning of it. Nazaire's used to being all alone. He knows how to handle it. But old too..."

Rex, the farm dog, was nibbling on his pants cuff and he didn't even notice. My father stood up. He was standing under the big, white fluorescent ceiling lights, smaller than usual, it seemed. He went over to the closet under the staircase and he put on his red checked jacket. But it wasn't cold outside. It was July. The big round clock on the wall was striking eleven.

He went toward the door, turned around and looked at us, the whole family around the table, the women braiding strips of cloth of all different colours to make rugs, and us kids on the floor in a corner, building a city and skyscrapers out of the fat phonebooks from the Vermont and New York Telephone Company. He looked at us and he left. On his own.

We waited. Five, ten minutes. But we were worried. We were thinking, all alone and old too. It was Paul who went out first, looking as if he was thinking about something else. We followed him.

It was a beautiful warm night. All the stars were out. We

43

heard thousands of frogs and insects in the ponds. Father was sitting in front of the brick fireplace on the lawn. He'd lit a big fire. He was staring at it, elbows on his knees.

"He's given us a good scare like this more than once, Nazaire has," he said.

We sat down all around him, on lawn chairs, on wooden crates, on the grass.

"We were beginning to get worried," my father said. "That summer was really hot. We couldn't sleep at night it was so hot. We went out on the porches of the houses, we sat down on the steps and we rolled cigarettes. It was 1914. Nazaire was seventeen and I was nineteen, almost twenty."

We pressed a little closer to him.

"We were beginning to get real worried," my father repeated. "It was at the end of the summer in 1914 and we were reading in the papers that the countries in Europe had declared war on each other. In those days we were a lot less educated. Europe was much further away. It was so far we wondered if we should believe it. For us fellows in Nicolet, Europe was a little like a fairy tale. For instance, once an apostolic delegate came to Nicolet. A personal representative of the Pope, with an Italian name of course. He celebrated a pontifical Mass at the cathedral. He pronounced a sermon. Afterward, our bishop spoke to thank him for his visit and entrust him with a message: go tell the Holy Father that we, in Nicolet, that we have faith. Because, you know, for us the Holy Father was a little like the Good Lord. We knew he existed but we never saw him and we knew we never would. Make sure you tell him that we believe, we faithful of Nicolet, even if we know we'll never see him."

A few of us giggled. My father didn't hear it.

"There are so many things," he said, "that you don't see but that are true just the same. So many things you don't understand. It's all darkness, like the night, yet everything is there. But you can't see a thing."

And he bent over to put a log on the fire.

"It was like with the papers," my father went on. "We wondered

44

if we should believe everything that was written in them. Especially since the news was frightening! They were talking about things we didn't know about, places and people we'd never heard of. The papers back in those days were *La Presse* and *Le Devoir* from Montreal. Newspapers that still exist in Canada. With advertisements for Bélanger wood stoves.

"People who didn't take the papers listened to the ones who did talk about the events. What was written was becoming more and more confusing. Confusing and troubling. Think about it: the Archduke Ferdinand of Austria-Hungary was assassinated by a Serbian. Austria-Hungary declared war on Serbia, then a little later, all of a sudden, like cannon shots, Germany declared war on Russian and France, then England on Germany. A couple days later, Austria-Hungary declared war on Russia, Serbia on Germany, and then France and England on Austria-Hungary. Imagine what we must have thought about all that, us fellows from Nicolet. Most of us had never gone further than the railway bridge! We understood it was like a free-for-all and we wondered who would be smart enough to stop first. But still, brawls were nothing new to us, we had them almost every Saturday night at the Hôtel Lambert with the fellows from La Baie du Febvre. We fought with all our heart until the Chief of Police came, an enormous man whose name was Léger, Léger Crochetière. But over there, in Europe, we wondered if there was a chief of police to stop the battle between all those countries we didn't even know about."

My father stopped talking because the sheriff just pulled up. We'd seen him coming in the distance along the road, with his red cherry lit up on the roof of his car. He always does that, especially at night, to act important. He pulled into the yard at top speed, got out, left his door open, looked at us for a moment around the fire, then he walked slowly toward us.

He said to my father, "I called the State Police. They'll be here tomorrow morning. I don't feel like spending the rest of the week walking through the woods."

"You know what you have to do," answered my father. "Where there's life, there's hope. Back in '14, we were plenty glad it was fall. We told ourselves the war would never reach us because of the winter. You know, back in those days, you didn't travel in the winter. Especially not from Europe to Canada. Suddenly we felt safe, hidden away on the American continent. But we were a little worried deep down all the same. We said to ourselves that anything was possible with people like that."

"Still telling war stories!" said the sheriff, bending over my father and putting his hand on his shoulder.

My father didn't answer. He raised his eyes to Heaven and sighed.

"I'd just started working at the glasses factory," my father went on. "Back then you didn't make much. Five dollars a week, no more. For five dollars, you worked from seven in the morning to six at night. You didn't complain. You figured you were lucky to have a job. For me it was different: I could have earned a living at my father's factory but I wanted to fend for myself for a while. We were poor but we weren't unhappy for all that. Life was simpler in those days. We'd leave the factory, run home and pick up the dinner that Mother had packed for us, then we'd grab our fishing tackle and set out on the Monteux road. We crossed the railway bridge. You had to be careful because that was the time the Montreal train came in. But we got a kick out of racing the train. More than once we'd reach the other side just in time. We used to say we had no time to lose, that the fish wouldn't wait, that it was the best time for walleye, but deep down we just liked to scare ourselves. On the other side was the wilderness, paradise for hunting and fishing. A man who knew how to go about it could bring back at least one deer in the fall. In the summer we caught two or three walleye every evening, three-pound walleye, and a pike from time to time, but those fish cut your line. Plenty of perch too. It was a good time. I used to fish with your uncle Eugène. My other brothers distrusted him a little because he was my father's right hand man at the factory. But I liked fishing with him because I learned what was going on at the factory when we talked. I've always liked to know what's going on."

He fell silent. Above us in the starry sky, an airplane flew over silently, with its two little lights. My father turned to my mother and my sister Rita.

"Bring us something to drink."

He lit a cigarette that made one more star in the night.

"Once we reached the Monteux," he said, "we used to meet Nazaire almost every evening. Nazaire spent all day in the woods. He didn't work. He'd lend a hand at the factory from time to time but you couldn't count on him. He was there one minute and not the next. You'd turn around and he'd be gone. You were talking to the air. Nazaire spent most of his time in the woods. When we met up with him almost every evening in the Monteux, we'd ask him, What did you do today? He tilted his head and looked at us like he didn't understand the question. He'd say, Nothing. I didn't do anything, I fished all day. We'd ask him, Did you catch anything? He'd answer, I fished all day but I didn't catch anything because the water was too warm. And Eugène and I, we wondered what he'd been doing all day. Deep down it was simple: he was dreaming. We really didn't know what he was dreaming about but we imagined they must have been important things. To make fun of him a little, we called him the Philosopher. When we got to the Monteux we said to him, Hello there, Philosopher. He looked at us with his surprised expression. He smiled. Now you're going to think he was stupid. He was a simple man, a simple man trying to understand and solve the world's big problems. That made him a little sad."

"You shouldn't criticize people behind their back," my mother said as she came back to serve the straight whisky in paper cups.

At our place we wash straight whisky down with a beer. It's called a chaser.

"I'm not criticizing him," my father answered. "I'm saying he was a philosopher."

"Some kind of a hermit!" the sheriff said.

We realized he was still around, and his motor was still running in the yard. In spite of it, the silence was growing heavy among us. We were thinking of the philosopher, all alone in the night.

"Nazaire never was like other men," my father went on. "We'd meet up with him in the Monteux, my brother Eugène and I. We had a spot of our own on the rocks by an old mill dam, with sink holes and eddies, perfect for walleye. We sat down and threw our lines in the water. Nobody said anything for a few minutes, then Nazaire began asking questions. Eugène said, Keep quiet, the fish are going to hear you. But Nazaire needed to know everything. He asked us questions we couldn't answer. He always was like that."

"That summer," my father went on, "Nazaire wanted to know why war had been declared between the countries in Europe. We hadn't gone to school too long and we hadn't listened too well. But he was even worse; he'd missed every other day. None of us knew history or geography. But we didn't want to admit we didn't know any more than Nazaire, not much more in any case. So we invented a little to keep from looking too ignorant. We used to say, The King of Germany wants to conquer the world like Julius Caesar back in history. And Nazaire would get mad. Can you tell me why they didn't lock him up while there was still time? Madmen ought to be locked up! But it's too late now! The damage is done! And Nazaire would light himself a cigarette like an expert. He'd just started smoking in those days and he'd grown a little mustache. He always had a mustache, Nazaire did. The one he has today is the same one he had back in those days, a little thicker, that's all. We were fishing. He leaned over to me and said in a low voice to keep from bothering Eugène who'd forbidden us to talk, he said, I'd like to get a hold of him, that old king of Germany.

"One evening Eugène brought the paper in his pail with his dinner. We sat down on the rocks, threw our lines in the water, then Eugène began talking as if no one had ever mentioned keeping quiet while fishing. First, there's no such thing as the king of Germany, he said, he's the Kaiser. And he showed us the Kaiser's picture in the paper. Nazaire said he looked like the priest who'd come to preach the Lent sermons the year before. As a matter of fact, the Kaiser did look nasty with his big mustache and his pointed helmet, his scheming eyes, and one arm shorter than the other. We figured that might have been why he was so bad. But in Nicolet there was Antoine who'd had his arm cut off, and he was the kindest man in the world. One thing was sure: the Kaiser wanted to run off with the world like a thief.

"Think about it: three fellows from Nicolet sitting on the rocks in the Monteux. We didn't know anything and we were trying to get some idea of what was going to happen. We said to each other, You can be sure the Kaiser has only one thing in mind: invading the world. Why? To get rich. But we'd been told that Europe was poor, and that the richest country in the world was the United States. So we drew some conclusions: it was no accident that the Kaiser wanted to invade the poor countries in Europe. He had big plans for the future and we saw what he was up to. He didn't want them in his way when he struck his big blow. And the big blow was the United States, you didn't have to speak Latin to understand that! And Nazaire said, If war ever breaks out in the States, we're finished here in Canada. Think about it: three fellows from Nicolet discussing the fate of the world, sitting on the rocks in the Monteux. Already we saw the Germans landing on the Plains of Abraham in Quebec City. The Plains of Abraham was the only battlefield we knew in Canada. That's where our ancestors had been beaten by the English. Eugène said, At least the English left us our language and our religion. I answered, Sure, but we stayed poor too. Whatever happens, said Eugène, if the Germans invade us, this time we'll lose everything. We didn't even know what religion the Germans were. What we did know was that they killed the men, raped the women and abandoned the children, and that they burned and pillaged everything. We were discussing those kind of things, but we quickly realized we shouldn't talk about them too much in front of Nazaire. He was getting nervous, he didn't know where to put his feet, he scratched his head, he dropped his line, he jumped for no reason—he was afraid, that was obvious. Enough that we had to comfort him, tell him not to worry, that we were far away in Canada, that winter was coming and that the war would never reach this far during the winter. We said to him, The Kaiser's not crazy enough to sail into the frozen Gulf with his boats. We used to say that but, deep down, we were looking forward to winter setting in.

"And then there were other things to think about. Winter really was coming and back in those days, as it came closer, we prepared ourselves like for a battle. The women—my mother, the aunts and my sisters—had already started knitting sweaters, tuques and mitts of all colours, and mending the Penman's longjohns we wore under our clothes. My father's wildcat coat had been taken out of mothballs and hung on the clothesline for a few days to air out. His *ceinture fléchée* too. During that time, us boys were bringing in the wood. Twenty cords of wood that had spent the summer outside. We brought them in during the fall and they dried out in the cellar all winter while we burned the wood from the year before. Then we started putting up the double windows on the rooms downstairs, then on the bedrooms upstairs and on the bull's-eye window in the attic. Next we caulked each of these windows with all the bits of cloth that had been kept all year for that, slips, towels worn threadbare, old sheets. My father had bought his pig from a farmer. The pieces of salted meat had been buried in sawdust in a shed attached to the house. Same thing for the carrots and beets. Sacks of potatoes and cabbages and tobacco hanging from the ceiling. War or no war, you couldn't forget anything if you wanted to get through the winter. And in the evening, when the gusty autumn winds stripped all the leaves from the trees, we sat around the wood stove. We'd never felt so good and never looked forward to winter so much. We were like bear cubs in their hole. Our happiness would have been complete if Eugène hadn't read us the paper: 18,000 Canadian soldiers were going to the front; the Government was asking Canadians to contribute to the war effort; Canada offered to send troops to England to defend her. We felt safe in the heart of our winter and we were thinking it over. We said to ourselves, if it goes on like this, their war will finish all by itself. There won't be anybody left to fight it. Nobody but old men, women and children. We sat up in the big kitchen, by the light of the oil lamps, and we waited for it to pass. One time, I remember, Nazaire said, Whatever happens, if the war ever comes here, you can always count on me."

During the course of that night, when my father got the story of Nazaire off his chest and told his big secret, we were all sitting around him before the fire. The night was pitch-black; the stars had hidden. It must have been after midnight. All of a sudden my mother and my sister reminded us kids that it was time to go up to bed. I knew I had no choice, it was no use protesting. So I went upstairs, lay down, waited until my mother went downstairs, then I unhooked the screen as I'd often done. I crept to the edge of the porch roof and lay down flat on my stomach. I was crosswise above the circle that had formed around my father. He was facing me without seeing me. His face was burning with the same glow as the fire.

What I heard and what I understood that night, even if I didn't hear or understand everything, marked me deeply enough that I took a dangerous stand of my own ten years later. If I became a draft dodger, it was partly because of what happened that night. Maybe I didn't understand everything with my head, but I can tell you that, lying flat on my stomach on the porch roof, I felt the earth turning through space and I discovered I was pretty small. The earth was turning through space with my father, Nazaire and me on it. Later I found I'd been wrong. Every man is alone on this earth. And I acted accordingly.

"You have to understand," my father said. "Nazaire wasn't crazy and he wasn't a coward. He was a loner—there's no madness in that. A man has the right to live his life like he wants to. It belongs to him, right? Nazaire was determined and brave. So determined that, the following spring, he upped and disappeared. In the spring of 1915, we were still in the middle of the war and we knew that this war would be a long one. It had gotten worse all winter. They'd dug trenches and faced each other without really knowing how to get out of it."

"They didn't know how to fight!" the sheriff said. "Back in World War Two—"

"Keep quiet!" Willy said sharply. "Don't you see we don't want to listen to your stories? Now keep quiet!"

"You," said the sheriff, turning to Willy, "you'd be better off going to bed. Save your strength, you're going to need it tomorrow. I think I'm going to go to bed too. See you tomorrow!"

And he went down the road in a cloud of dust, the red cherry lit up on his roof.

"Poor fool," my father murmured. He was silent a little while, then he began his story again. "The next spring, Nazaire disappeared. We had no idea where he'd gone. He didn't have any friends, he didn't go out with girls, nobody he could have confided in. It was in March, when the ice breaks up. And, as far as anybody could remember, there hadn't ever been a break-up like that one. In those days they didn't break up the ice like they do today. The river froze from one bank to the other. Beautiful blue ice as high as a man. The ice breaks, then piles up. It forms ice jams that can last for weeks. During that time, the water was climbing. Port Saint-François was completely flooded. Port Saint-François is a beach, a half-hour by wagon from Nicolet. That was where the well-off people of Nicolet used to spend their summers. The others went there to swim on the weekends. Back then, several years before, there had been a real village at Port Saint-François, but a big break-up had washed everything away. There was nothing left but a large unpainted house on the hillside. My father had bought it to make himself a cottage. We took the wagon and hitched it up to go see the water and the ice. We rode along the road as long as the water stayed below the edge of the wagon. The horse balked: he was afraid. We saw my father's cottage in the distance. There was water halfway up the downstairs windows. We wanted to go there, save some furniture, tie up the little woodshed that was floating behind and in danger of drifting away, but the current was too strong and there were ice blocks floating past. We had a lot of trouble turning the wagon around without spilling, and once we were on dry land, the horse snorted and shook like a big dog and almost upset us."

"If it was me, I wouldn't have been afraid to go there," my sister Rita said.

"You," replied Willy, "you're like Nazaire. You never do anything like anybody else!"

"I would have walked on the ice," Rita answered.

"If we didn't go there, that's because it was impossible," my father cut in. And he continued, "One afternoon, in the last days of April, we were finally able to go to the cottage. There was an enormous ice-floe that had come to rest against the front of the house. We climbed on top of it and looked around. When we raised our eyes, we saw the barrcl of a rifle pointing at us from one of the upstairs windows. It was Nazaire! He asked, Are you all alone? We answered yes and he lowered the rifle. We stood there, frozen. We couldn't get over it. Then Nazaire said, There's a ladder around the side. We climbed up and went in through the window. Nazaire was there in the front room, the girls' room, with his supplies scattered everywhere, empty water jugs, a sack of flour, some salt pork too, in a wooden butter crate. He had a real woodsman's beard and he was staring at us. Finally he asked, Tell me honestly if the war is here. We told him no. He didn't seem to believe us. He said, I'd rather stay here; I don't want to go to war. We explained the best we could, but he didn't want to understand. The war is still in Europe, Eugène said, it won't come here. They're much too busy fighting over there. We asked Nazaire what he would have done if the war had broken out here. He answered, I would have fired on the soldiers. I wouldn't have let anybody come near. Eugène asked again, What have you been doing all this time? Nazaire explained, I settled in the best I could. I couldn't light a fire: the stove is under water downstairs. I froze to death. During the day I went up on the roof to warm myself in the sun. One night I heard terrible cracking noises. The wind was blowing a full gale.

I was afraid the cottage would be carried away by the water, the ice and the wind. I went up on the roof and climbed into the big oak. I brought supplies and a blanket. I stayed in the tree two days. Have you gone crazy? asked Eugène who was beginning to get angry. Nazaire looked at us peacefully. No, I'm not crazy. I was afraid, that's all. I was freezing in my tree but I didn't dare go back into the cottage. I was afraid of being carried away. During my two days in the tree, I whittled a whole branch, look. We went over to the window. Nazaire had carved a whole branch, twice as long as my arm, along its entire length, from the trunk almost to the end. As if little figures had sprung to life on the naked white branch.

"It kept me company, Nazaire said. And he added, I found a little dog too. I saw him swimming from up here, then he climbed onto the ice pretty far up from the cottage. I wondered where he could have come from. He was howling. I called him and he was howling. I threw him some cracker crumbs to attract him. I climbed down the ladder as far as the water. I called him and he was howling. In the end he jumped into the water to come and join me. I was happy. I brought the little dog into the room. I fed him but he brought everything up. He died during the night. He must have gotten too cold or gone too long without eating. I kept him, he's in there. And Nazaire lifted the top of a cardboard box. The little dog was there, his hair all matted and his teeth white. Eugène went to Nazaire's side and put his hand on his shoulder. He led him to the bed. They were sitting side by side and Eugène was holding Nazaire by the shoulder. He was rocking him gently. He said, Don't worry, Nazaire, don't worry about anything. Nothing will happen to you. If anything ever happens, I'll be there. I won't leave you alone. Understand? I won't leave you alone. Nazaire looked at Eugène, astonished. He nodded his head. Then all three of us went back in the rowboat."

"All the same," said my father, "Nazaire wasn't a coward, and he wasn't afraid either. He had only one fear: the war. As for the rest, he was like everybody else, a young man of seventeen, a little timid, perhaps, but that's the way it was in those days."

He stood up to turn over the big log in the fire. Thousands of sparks flew up and lit the faces in a circle around the fireplace. We heard a dog barking at the Bradleys' place. Sometimes a car came down the road; we made out its headlights, then the sound and the dust faded away.

"It was back in those days," my father went on, "the same year, if I remember rightly, in the spring of 1915. Nazaire had come back to the house, and he'd started working at the factory with Father and my other brothers. Except for what we were hearing about the war, everything had gone back to normal. Every evening after supper we read the papers, but otherwise we tried not to think about it. We lit big grass fires to revive the earth, and we dug the garden and Mother's flowerbeds in the yard. A few fishing trips too, now and again. Perch tastes better in cold water. We were leading our quiet little lives. One night, it must have been in early June, we were woken up by the siren. We got dressed in a hurry and went down to the kitchen. Nazaire hadn't even taken the time to put on his pants. He was wearing his nightshirt. He ran past us without seeing us and dived down the basement stairs. Meanwhile the neighbours, who'd seen our lights, came into the kitchen and announced that the big convent was on fire. My mother and my sisters began crying, standing together by the stove. We had only one thought in mind: to get to the fire as quickly as possible and lend a hand. Before we left, my father took me by the arm and led me downstairs. We found Nazaire curled up at the bottom of the coalbin, his nightshirt all dirty. Then my father, who was a calm man and never raised his voice, began shouting in a way I'd never heard before. Would you get out of there, you good-for-nothing! It's not the war, it's a fire! The big convent's on fire! If you can't act like a man, then go up to bed! And try not to cry so loud, you'll frighten your mother and your sisters! I was humiliated for him. Nazaire got to his feet and tried to wipe off his nightshirt, but he got it even dirtier with his sooty hands. Then he went up to the kitchen without a word. We went off to the fire without waiting any longer. The convent was near the cathedral, on the main street. It was a large stone building that had been constructed about fifteen years earlier, I think. That's why we called it the big convent, to distinguish it from the older, smaller one that stood next to it. When we arrived, the students and nuns were all on the lawn. Three hundred ghosts in white nightdresses and bonnets, crying out in despair. The flames were leaping from the windows with an uncontrollable fury. We heard the fire roaring in the classrooms. It was so hot we couldn't get any closer than a hundred feet. The fire was going so well we said to ourselves we'd never be able to put it out. We were sure the entire convent would burn. The volunteer firemen finally pulled up with their horses and their hoses. They worked the pump as hard as they could but the water pressure wasn't high enough to reach the top floors. The Chief of Police, Léger Crochetière, was there, along with the chief of the volunteer firemen, a man named Boucher. He was so unnerved that he shouted contradictory orders at everybody. Finally, since nobody seemed to be paying attention to him, he went after the students, the nuns and us spectators. He wanted to make us move back. But we were far enough as it was; the fire was so hot we couldn't get any closer. He drove us back, pushing and shoving. He was vulgar with everybody, even the nuns. That was his way of putting out the fire. My father began talking loud too, and they had just about come to blows, he and Boucher, when a great clamour rose from the crowd. The convent chaplain had just appeared at a front window. It was right at the top; the fire hadn't reached that high. We wondered how we could get a ladder up there. But the chaplain began shouting something then he disappeared inside, where the smoke must have been thick enough to suffocate a man in two minutes. Later we discovered why. The firemen there heard him say he was going to get the Holy Sacrament. When we saw him go back inside, we knew right away he'd never come out alive. But we could do nothing to rescue him. The fire was too hot and the smoke too thick; nobody would have ventured inside. But just then a man came running out of the crowd, went by us without saying a word, pushed aside a fireman who tried to stop him and entered the convent through the main door where a torrent of smoke was escaping. That man who we hadn't recognized had had the courage to enter the inferno to save the chaplain. We were sure we'd never see either of them again. We were too moved to speak. And each of us was already picturing the two charred corpses that would be dragged from the wreckage once the fire was out. Then the crowd surged toward the courtyard. People pressed around something or somebody. We came nearer, my father, my brothers and I. People were saying, He just came out the little courtyard door. He's there. We don't know which one it is, the chaplain or the other. I pushed and shoved my way to the front. It was Nazaire! Completely black, in his shorts, his hair and eyebrows singed. Lying at the foot of a tree, out of breath, almost unable to speak. Yet he managed to say over and over, I saw him! I saw him! He was in the flames! I saw him, he was going over to the other side! I shouted, he didn't understand! He was going over to the other side! I saw him! He went into the flames then the ceiling fell in front of him! It was Nazaire!" my father repeated in a strong voice. "It was Nazaire who'd had the courage to enter the convent to try to save the chaplain. My father was crying as he looked at him—I'd never seen that before. We carried him to the house. His hair and eyebrows were singed. His mustache had gone up too. He didn't speak; he'd swallowed so much smoke he had trouble breathing. We laid him down on the couch in the parlour, we opened the window and my mother made us step back to give him air. Nazaire was like a hero, burned and out of breath. He had gone into the flames to try to save a man while the rest of us stayed on the lawn, watching. That was Nazaire, do you see? The same man we'd found curled up in the coalbin in his nightshirt an hour earlier. That's why I'm telling you," my father repeated, "that Nazaire was braver than all of us put together. He was afraid of the war, that's for sure, but he was a man in spite of it all. A man who wasn't like the rest: both more cowardly and more courageous than the rest."

My father coughed to clear his throat. It was as if the night was growing thicker. There were big red coals in the fireplace and my sister Rita threw a log on top. My father looked all around and said, "I'm going to bed. You should do the same if you want to get up early tomorrow morning. We'll continue the search tomorrow."

But my sister Rita stood up. She went over to Father, put her hands on his shoulders and held him firmly in his chair.

"We're not going to bed until you tell us why Nazaire ran away to the mountain. You know why and you don't want to tell us."

"What do you want me to tell you?"

"Why Nazaire went off to the mountain. There must be a reason! You just told us Nazaire was both cowardly and courageous. It takes a courageous man to go off all alone on the mountain at his age! Why?"

"Because there's a secret in Nazaire's life. A secret he's never told anybody, but that I know about."

"We can talk about it now."

"Maybe. Maybe we can since he's gone."

My father hesitated. He ran his fingers through his grey hair. He pounded his fist into his hand.

"Goddamn," he said, "it's simple enough, we just didn't want to go to war, Nazaire, Eugène and me! We didn't want to, understand? In those days we were less educated than we are today but there was one thing we did know: one living man is worth a thousand dead men. And we'd been taught since we were little that it's always better not to get mixed up in other people's business. You have to understand that: Canada isn't the United States. It's true today, and it was even truer back in those days. We didn't have any free world to defend! A little handful of people, hanging onto some pretty poor land, with six months of winter on the year. Canada is no Florida! We didn't have anything to go defend. Where was this war, eh? Who was there fighting it? On our side, I mean. France and England. Do you think we were about to go give our lives to defend those people? Do you think so? Goddamn, when our ancestors were fighting to

58

build the colony here, the French were happy to be bowing and scraping at the King's court! Then one fine day we lost the battle of the Plains of Abraham. Why? Because the French didn't even come and help us. Do you think we were about to go get ourselves killed for France? Especially since we stayed Catholic when the French wanted to throw out all their priests during the Revolution. After all, no use being more Catholic than the Pope! So you understand, there was no talk of going to defend France. Sure, but what about England, you'll say. It's England that the Canadian government wanted to help. It's mighty difficult to be for that. The proof is that us French Canadians didn't have one member in the Borden government in Ottawa. You have to admit we weren't on the same side! Besides, us French Canadians had been brought up to respect our traditions. Well, our traditions were to be faithful to the land. I can tell you that there were more than a few of us back in those days who'd never gone further than the end of their land. And I'd also say it was practically one of our traditions to be poor. We weren't ambitious people. We did with what we had. We'd already proved it when the United States wanted to revolt against England. People came looking to ask us to fight on their side. We never wanted to. You see, we didn't want to fight. We had enough work raising our big families and clearing rocks off our land! When there started to be talk of conscription in the spring of 1917, just about everybody was of the same mind: we had nothing to do with it. No business going to defend England, any more than France! That was somebody else's war, we had nothing to do with it. We'd been fighting our war for two hundred years against the rocks, the mosquitoes and the winter. Six months in the fields, six months in the lumber camps. Don't you think that's enough? We weren't cowards, we had plenty of guts! Our land was there to prove it! At the end of the summer of 1917, when the Borden government passed the law to force us to go to war, we felt like we'd just been betrayed one more time. What we did proves we weren't cowards!''

Up on my roof, I was beginning to catch a chill. I went inside to get myself a blanket and a pillow. I even went quietly

59

downstairs to the kitchen and got myself a supply of cookies. I set up my encampment on the porch roof, and it was almost as if I was outside of the world. My eyes turned toward the stars, I listened to a voice that seemed to come from beyond. All the places my father conjured up appeared in the sky among the twinkling stars.

Even today, at twenty-five, I wonder if what I know of Nazaire's story wasn't clearer to me that night, at fourteen, than after all the conversations I heard later and all the explanations that were given to me. But in the meantime, in a certain way, I've had the chance to become another Nazaire myself.

"To give you an idea," my father went on, "there was a man named François Desruisseaux. This man had some land on the Petit-Bois concession, on the Pierreville side. We found out through the papers what had happened. He was one hundred percent French Canadian; he had thirteen children. With his wife and his children, he slaved from sun-up to sun-down. That's how it was in those days. He must have had ten cows, a horse and some chickens. He was poor, but no more than the others, everybody was in those days. He was poor but he had plenty of guts. And he knew that if he went to war, everybody would starve to death back home. Most of all he knew that if he got killed in the war, his widow and children would be condemned to a life of poverty. This man was no coward, he was well built, big and tall, the strength of nature was in him. As the news came through and people talked about conscription, he got more and more worried. One morning his wife found him in the stable, sitting on the little milking stool, a rope in his hand. Another time in the shed with an axe—and not for cutting wood, you understand? Desruisseaux was more and more discouraged, and his wife too. I imagine they must have spent long evenings talking quietly in their bed while the children slept all around them. Autumn was coming. In Quebec in those days, people would go up to the lumber camps in the autumn. They were up north, much further than the end of the roads, where there was nothing but snow and wild animals. Trees too, all around. The men used to gather in Trois-Rivières at the beginning of September. That was where they took the train to La Tuque. La Tuque is a hundred miles north of Trois-Rivières. After that it's the forest, nothing more. But still, once they were there, the men had only travelled half way. There were roads through the forest, lumbering roads. There were horses, nothing but horses. The companies organized convoys for the men, materials and supplies. It took a week, a week and a half, sometimes two to reach the camps, depending on the place and the snow that was beginning to fall around that time. The camps were large, round wooden buildings. There were dormitories and another camp for the kitchen. And a separate camp for the foremen, of course. This man, François Desruisseaux, he'd gone to the camps in his youth like everybody else. He'd worked mostly at Consol's Camp 105. But he hadn't gone up there for a long time, because during the winter he found work with a fellow named Desnoyers who cut ice on the Saint-François River. In those days everybody had an icebox to keep their food cold in the summer, especially in the cities and towns. During the winter, some farmers sawed enormous blocks of ice and stored them in sheds, covered with sawdust, for the summer. François Desruisseaux would have continued with his little winter routine if the conscription rumours hadn't discouraged him once and for all. He must have agreed on it with his wife in their bed, because in September, the entire family headed up to Trois-Rivières. That was already quite a journey, and the Desruisseaux children had never gone that far. But there's more: this man put his whole family on the train for La Tuque. Each child carried something, a box, an old suitcase, a sack. They took only the essentials: clothes, blankets, some flour and salt pork. A few cooking utensils and some axes too. They set out with the loggers to La Tuque. That was already something to behold. In those days there weren't any children, let alone women, in the lumber camps. Think about it: one women with two hundred men in a camp all winter! That would have been enough to start the blood flowing. The loggers wondered where these people could have been going. Then the Desruisseaux family arrived at La Tuque. Right away they left the village behind and walked for a good hour, then they set up a sort of tent along side the road, made from a big canvas sheet stretched over the branches. They never even considered following the company convoys. The important thing was not to attract attention. They took a road that wasn't used any more, where nobody ever went. A road where the grass had already grown up again, with bushes here and there. The first night they camped a few miles from La Tuque. That much is known because some children saw them. Afterward, not a trace until next spring. Thanks to a trapper coming back down, we found out what had happened. He'd found them frozen to death in a camp abandoned several years before. They must have run out of supplies and fallen sick. They'd eaten wood and chewed their blankets. There were fourteen frozen corpses in the camp; five of the children were laid out on the table as if they had died first and had been put there. The others were in their beds. Thirteen children plus the father and the mother, that makes fifteen. One was missing; he must have left to try to find help. He was never found."

My father fell silent a moment, then said again, "You see what a man like Desruisseaux was ready to do to not go to war! It was more or less the same for all of us."

"One morning at the post office," my father went on, "we found out what was in store for us. It was around nine o'clock, a fine day in late August, I remember. There must have been fifty people on the street in front of the post office. Kids with their bicycles too. Courchesne the notary, in his black suit, was making a speech like some kind of politician. Five or six men were standing there listening. There was big Nestor Bourdon with his boots and the young fellows who usually hung around with him, Baptiste Métivier, Louis-Paul Deshaies, little Cantin, maybe Arthur Martin too—I don't recall now. But I do remember that Nazaire was there. I was sitting in the little flat wagon pulled by the grey horse that belonged to the glasses factory. It wasn't usually me who went, but that morning I was the one they sent to the post office and the station. Looking after the machines was my job. I'd worked with the company to set them up, and I knew them better than anybody. But that morning there must not have been any emergency repairs and the fellow who usually went must have been sick. There were already fifty people in front of the station, and more were coming. Abbé Poirier, the father superior at the Petit Séminaire, was there, and Madame Lambert, the hotel-keeper's wife. Everybody I used to run into was there, Ovide Proulx in his wagon too. Back then everybody in Nicolet and the rest of the parish knew each other. I remember I tied up my horse a little further away because of all the wagons in front of the post office. Little Cantin shouted to me, We're going to have to join the Army! It says so in the paper! Then I heard Courchesne the notary telling us we'd have to do our duty. Nestor Bourdon was already saying we'd get a chance to travel and see the world. Everybody was talking at once, like on the church steps after Mass. I walked through the crowd and went into the post office. Charles-Emile Lafond, who was about the same age as me, handed me the company mail and said, It doesn't bother me. If you work at the post office, you don't have to go."

My father paused, then went on in a low voice. "For a second I saw myself dressed up like a soldier with everybody else, lined up with the shortest in front and the tallest in back, like at school. We were marching down the street by the post office, and at the end of the street was the war. There was fire everywhere and houses falling down. Then I thought of my mother and I said to myself, I'm not going to war. I rode right back to the factory. It was the same story there. The men had gathered near the main office. The boss—someone named McDuff from the States—was talking. He said, If you're called, you'll have to do your duty. We'll get along without you, but don't worry, we're going to need manpower and we'll hire your wives and oldest daughters first. There'll be work for everybody. Nobody's going to starve. When you come back, your jobs will be waiting for you. Everything will go back to normal like before. We plan to keep on a few skilled workers. We'll take care of the formalities ourselves; they'll just have to sign the papers. We'll be having a meeting to pick the men who'll be staying. They'll be doing their duty in their own way by contributing to the war effort. Now go back to work."

Slowly, my father looked around at his listeners. He lit a cigarette and you could see his worried face in the glow from the match. And up on the roof, I understood what he was going through because I'd been drafted too.

"Let me tell you," my father went on in a low voice. "We already knew pretty well what was going to happen. Back then nobody would dare say what he was thinking out loud, but we can now. Nazaire's on the mountain. If he's dead, maybe he can hear us. If he's alive he can't, and maybe it's better that way. I don't have to tell you that when I left work that day, I went straight home. Eugène was on the steps with Nazaire. Joseph was there too, a neighbour who was a friend of Eugène's. I sat down next to them on the steps. We didn't talk. We were feeling bad and we were thinking it over: Nestor Bourdon will go for sure, it'll be his chance to see Europe. The notary won't— professionals are exempt. Little Cantin won't pass the medical. Big Courteau who's chicken like everybody knows—he'll go. Maybe Louis-Paul Deshaies, maybe not. And Joseph, Eugène's friend. Us three brothers, Eugène, Nazaire and me, they'll call us up too. But deep down, each of us was saying to himself, I won't go."

... So one September night in 1917, a man set out on foot with a big pack on his back. It was a fine mild night in early fall. He'd been walking for an hour and a half, maybe two. He'd left Nicolet on the little dirt road that winds through the big elms along the river. For a while the wooden sidewalks along the road kept him company like two rails in the night. Then the road straightened out. The trees stood alone in the fields. He quickened his pace. Say what you like, no matter how beautiful the night might be, it always gets to you. He was walking at a good clip, long enough to hear the sound of the water at the end of the road. It was a little like leaves rustling in the wind, only smoother. The road led to the water, and that water was the St. Lawrence River that runs through the whole province of Quebec. He reached Port Saint-François, near the beach where people went swimming in the summer. He was almost at the wharf where the boats used to dock in the days when they carried freight. They didn't use that dock much for shipping any more, but it was a fine place to go fishing or watch the sun set over the water.

He knew the place very well, but now he had to guess his way, because he couldn't see in the darkness. He stopped a few hundred feet before the dock. He touched the trees, felt his way with his foot, then he started down a little road, just wagon tracks and some grass in between. At the end, his outstretched hands met a wooden wall. It was a big cottage with six windows on the second floor, a very big frame house. He was there. He knew the key was under the mat. He went inside and lit a lamp. There was a big living room with wicker furniture; one end led into a dining room with a table big enough to seat a dozen people.

He put down his things and sat in a chair to listen to his breathing. Nothing stirred; he was all alone. Just the breeze and the night outside. A little later he blew out the lamp and set out again on the road. He retraced his steps back to Nicolet and went into the house on the main street. He came out a moment later with another pack on his back. He made the same trip three times that night. The last time, when he got back to Port Saint-François, the first light of dawn was beginning to sketch out the little willows to the east.

Nazaire unpacked his things in the girls' room upstairs, like the last time. He set everything out around the bed, pushed the heavy chest of drawers against the door and lay down with his clothes on. He spent a long time staring at the ceiling, listening to the wind in the big oak tree, then he fell asleep.

The notices had started arriving at the Nicolet Post Office. Every morning, young fellows would come out with a black look

65

on their faces and an envelope in their hands. You knew what that meant. Two or three days later, you saw them get on the train to Montreal. Some days there were five or six. They pretended they didn't care, laughing and calling to each other, When the Army doctors see you naked, they'll send you back home under armed guard!

Some of them did everything in their power to get sick a few days before the medical. People said if you walked around with a blotter in your shoe for three or four days, that would do the trick. It didn't happen in our town, but we heard about some who'd cut off a hand, a finger or a toe.

Some mothers took their grown sons to the station, and they were crying. Big fellows, twenty years old, crying in their mothers' arms!

Everybody was called to the medical. As you might expect, it was in Montreal. The Army doctors were at the end of a big hall, surrounded by their instruments. All the conscripts took off their clothes and lined up, naked, not saying a thing. Silence. It lasted five minutes, not a second more. When you finished, you got dressed and you knew from the doctors' look whether you'd be called or not. But you didn't understand a thing because the doctors spoke English.

Around seven in the evening, when the Montreal train arrived in Nicolet, there were always a lot of people at the station. Some were laughing, others crying. But some of them were ready to tear the place apart. They shouted right there on the station platform, Just let them try and get me! They'll see! I'll be waiting for them!

And they pointed their fingers as if they had a gun. And as it turned out, they usually disappeared in the next few days. Nobody knew exactly where they were, but in Nicolet and the countryside, everybody had his own idea. They just said to themselves, If I were a deserter...

First came the notices in the mail. What could the deserters' families say? Even in the family nobody knew where the deserter had hidden. In the evening by lamplight, they spent hours reading the piece of paper over and over again, shaking

66

their heads. Then one fine day the soldiers arrived. Five or six of them in their khaki uniforms would get off at the station, speaking English among themselves. They walked all through the town to make their presence known, then they went and knocked on the deserter's door. Usually his parents told the truth: they didn't know where he was.

Then the soldiers took rooms at the hotel and conducted an investigation for a day or two. They questioned everybody—in the street, at the post office, the restaurant, the hotel. They went to see the priest and they went to see the mayor, but above all they paid a visit to Courchesne the notary.

Courchesne was very fat and he always wore an impeccable black suit like an undertaker. He used to tap his belly and say, A man with nothing on his conscience has nothing to hide. His office was at the corner of Notre Dame Street in a big, white three-storey house that he owned. Nobody ever knew everything that went on in that office, but the people in Nicolet discovered the notary took an interest in almost everything. For instance, he'd meet somebody on the main street after supper and say to him, So you've been called up, eh, Julien? Come see me tomorrow in my office. I just might be able to do something for you.

My father said Courchesne the notary squealed on the conscripts to the soldiers. Nobody could prove it, but you'd have to be blind not to see it.

It happened to a fellow named Lemire from La Baie du Febvre. He'd heard that Courchesne could fix all kinds of things. He'd just been called up for his medical, and as you might expect, he didn't want to join the Army. On Thursday he was at the notary's office. On Friday he was in uniform and starting training.

Lemire told us later how it happened. The notary was as kind as he could be. He was smoking a fat cigar and he even offered one to Lemire. But Lemire didn't feel like smoking a cigar, and he filled his pipe with strong tobacco instead. Then the notary slyly made him talk and admit he was planning to desert, but Lemire wouldn't tell him where he was thinking of

67

hiding. So, leaning forward with his fat white hands resting on the blotter, clutching his cigar, the notary started talking about the medical. He said to Lemire, If I remember right, you were always a little weak in the lungs. Lemire didn't have to be asked twice, and he even managed to cough a little, it seems, to convince the notary. Courchesne wrote something down on a scrap of paper and told Lemire that things could be worked out. Then he got the conversation around to a plot of land Lemire owned that was right in the middle of Caya's property, and it so happened Courchesne and this Caya were doing business at the time. But Lemire would have nothing to do with it. Finally the notary stood up and slapped him on the back and sent him off with a big smile.

When he got to the examining room in Montreal, Lemire was as nervous as all get-out. A rough fifteen minutes and that's it, he told himself. But things didn't turn out quite the way he expected: he spent almost a year at the front. The soldiers led him to a little room off to the side and the doctor gave him a quick examination. Then they gave him a uniform and that night he slept in the camp. Some examination for a man with bad lungs!

Don't forget that Courchesne the notary was the chairman of the Nicolet exemption board. The government set up these boards to review the applications of men who thought they had good reasons not to obey their conscription notices. First there were those whose jobs were essential to the proper running of the wartime economy—skilled workers, for example. Plus a few special cases who had family reasons.

Professionals were automatically exempt. Notaries, lawyers and pharmacists weren't conscripted. In other words, they recruited the soldiers from the workers and farmers. Some people muttered that it wasn't fair.

Some of the private conversations in the notary's office were about exemptions. The poor buggers who had every reason in the world not to go and fight talked to Courchesne a few days before appearing at the Courthouse in front of the exemption board. They said the notary took pay-offs there too, but you couldn't prove that either.

And just like with the medical, a conscript would be very surprised to find himself in uniform, in spite of the notary's fine promises. But what could he do? After all, he couldn't say he'd paid off the notary to fix things! The luckier ones managed to disappear in time; the rest got a free trip across the water.

My father was one of those who'd been appointed to the glasses factory as a skilled worker. He was the man who knew the machinery best. They needed him to keep it running and fix it, so he'd received his exemption papers. He always had to carry them on him; he could have been asked to show them at any time.

It was a troubled time. With his big belly and his little legs, Courchesne the notary was always conducting an investigation. He knew everybody, of course. He had the list of conscripts, and he knew who hadn't answered the call. He knew the families— fathers, mothers, brothers, sisters, wives and children. He seemed profoundly concerned with what happened to everybody. He was everywhere—at the station, the post office, the Hôtel Lambert and the Restaurant Central.

It was at the restaurant that he spent most of his time. Before the war, he used to come there from time to time, but in 1917, he was there every day, an hour in the morning, an hour in the afternoon and sometimes even at night. His black suit contrasted strangely with the checked shirts and the rough twill of the regulars. At the time, people didn't notice it right away, but the more the notary stayed at the Restaurant Central, the more soldiers came to spend a few days in Nicolet. That must have been in October or November.

We saw him at the same table with people like Ti-noir Côté, Rouge, M. Gendron, Ephrem Laporte too, and some-times, but less often, Alphonse Descôteaux. Some company for a notary to keep, especially Descôteaux. Because those people, you might as well admit, were the good-for-nothings in Nicolet and thereabouts. Notorious loafers, petty thieves and poachers from father to son. The dregs.

And those people had only one subject of conversation: the deserters. They seemed very interested in the fate of the men who'd disappeared. They all had their theories. For instance, they'd say, take Fred Lampron—I wouldn't be surprised if he went to hide out in his father-in-law's sugar shack. The notary nodded his head with a Hmmm! And the next day, we heard that shots had been fired on Fred Lampron's father-in-law's land.

That happened maybe a dozen times, and soon people stopped talking to each other. They got suspicious over nothing. Nobody trusted anybody. Old friends didn't even say hello any more when they met. Every man for himself, and every man alone!

They said some of the deserters' families had given in to threats and blackmail and denounced their own people. It's not unlikely. Remember back then, in a small town like Nicolet, everybody knew each other. You knew just about everything about everybody, even the most secret things, and that made people vulnerable. That's why from time to time we'd hear about a deserter who'd been captured.

Life went on feverishly, day and night. You'd meet wagons without their lights on the road. People on foot on all the paths. Sometimes in the middle of the day, in the distance you'd see the figure of a woman silhouetted against the frozen fields.

That was wartime! But there was another war, right in Nicolet, between the people themselves.

In his father's cottage in Port Saint-François, Nazaire was as quiet as a bear holed up for the winter. Day and night, he kept his fur cap pulled over his ears, his hands in his big leather mitts and his *ceinture fléchée* pulled tightly around his cloth coat. But still he froze. He'd spend the whole day in bed with the brightly coloured quilts pulled up over his head. He froze because he couldn't light a fire during the day; someone could have seen or smelled the smoke. He only lit a fire at night. After nightfall, he went down to the kitchen and got the stove going. It was still risky, but it had to be done. He nailed boards across the two kitchen windows from the inside. He bolted the door carefully and put an old rug in front of the crack so nobody outside could see the firelight. Then he'd sit by the stove, dozing for an hour or two.

One night he heard footsteps outside in the dead leaves. There wasn't any snow yet—it must have been early November. He was dozing off and he woke with a start because he thought he'd heard steps. He listened. The blood pounded in his ears. That's what it was. He picked up his hunting rifle, an old 12 gauge that was always loaded, and crept silently out of the kitchen. He went into the big living room at the front of the house and he waited.

The footsteps were circling the house. Nazaire was afraid; cold sweat was pouring down his back. He was afraid, but he still kept his finger on the 12's trigger and he was determined to fire. The steps climbed up to the door. Nazaire shouldered the rifle. A voice called, Anyone there? Silence. Nazaire trained his gun on the door. The voice called, Anyone there? Open up, it's Jos Blanchette! Nazaire didn't answer. He didn't even breathe. He crept toward the door, three steps from the voice outside. Open up, it's Jos Blanchette!

Then it happened so quickly Nazaire didn't even have time to fire. Before he knew it, there was someone behind him, sticking a rifle barrel in his back. Nazaire turned around slowly, his hands in the air like in the Westerns. There was a young man in his twenties with a huge black beard. Drop your rifle, he said. We aren't going to hurt you. Nazaire put his rifle on the wicker chair and the man went to open the door. In walked another who looked just like him.

They said who they were: the two Blanchette brothers. They'd hidden out in the Manseaus' sugar shack at the other end of Port Saint-François, to keep out of the Army too, of course. At first they stayed in the shack, then they started looking around, especially at night. That's how they smelled the smoke from Nazaire's fire. They knew right away that there was a deserter like them in the house, but they couldn't figure out

71

who it was. So they just decided to have a look.

The three men sat around the stove. As they talked, Nazaire found out there were at least eight deserters in Port Saint-François. There was even one in the big lighthouse on the beach.

The Blanchette brothers talked about pooling their supplies and organizing a patrol, but Nazaire wouldn't hear of it. He said everybody would be better off on his own. If one of us gets caught, he explained, we won't all be caught together.

It happened a while later, one night when the snow had begun to fall. Nazaire was sitting in front of the fire, his eyes closed. He was picturing the big white flakes and that made him think of Christmas when he was a child. A feeling of comfort was numbing him, when suddenly he heard gunshots from Port Saint-François. He quickly put out the fire with the supply of sand he kept by the stove. He took up position behind the door with his gun and he waited. He kept watch till morning, but nothing happened. Then he climbed up in the oak to get a good look around. Nothing. There was beautiful white snow everywhere, but not a single footprint. But still, Nazaire stayed in the tree most of the day.

Then that night, the same routine as before. Footsteps outside the cottage. Open up, it's Blanchette! Nazaire let him in, and Blanchette told him that the soldiers had come the night before. They'd walked along the beach to the other end of Port Saint-François and begun searching the sugar shacks, one by one. The Blanchette brothers had seen the whole thing from the top of a tall pine tree. But when the soldiers disappeared from sight at the edge of the Manseaus' woods, they'd heard one shot, then others, close together. Then silence. Not a trace of the soldiers. The Blanchettes wondered where they could have gone.

In the morning, the Blanchette brothers wanted to warn Nazaire, but it had snowed all night and they would have left footprints. They'd waited until the end of the next day, since it had started snowing again and it looked as though it would go on all night and cover their tracks.

They didn't know who'd fired. They didn't know either if anybody had been hit. Or if anybody had been caught. What they did know was that the soldiers would come back, and that was why the Blanchettes began talking about organizing patrols again. But Nazaire didn't want any part of it.

"I'd like to help you," he said, "But I don't want to risk it. I wish you didn't even know I was here. The best thing for a deserter is to lie low. But this is the second time you've been here. It's dangerous."

Then he pulled his fur cap to one side to show them he was serious. But the Blanchette brothers weren't about to give up. They left, telling Nazaire to think it over carefully, and saying they'd come back for his answer in a few days.

But the next day Nazaire was gone. He'd taken everything with him. Not one sign of his stay in the cottage in Port Saint-François. Meanwhile, Eugène had just been called up, and he'd disappeared too. The two brothers had vanished into the Canadian winter.

It was a time of malice and revenge. People who'd known each other for years and years didn't even say a word when they met. When they did open their mouths, it was only to torture each other with insinuations. Listen here, just where *are* those two boys of yours? Seems to me we never saw them in soldiers' clothes. They must have joined up pretty quick! And the other man would answer, If I were you, I wouldn't talk so loud. Go ask your son-in-law what he thinks. They say you've started sugaring-off in the middle of winter! Some people saw smoke coming out of your shack last week.

Usually these mutual threats did the trick. Scaring each other was a game, and they were good at it. Everybody knows the French Canadians love a good quarrel. They're always in court over broken fences or cows let loose in the neighbour's fields. They couldn't change their ways, even in wartime. But the deserters' families never denounced each other. It would have never stopped, like when you pull on a loose end in a piece of knitting. The deserters threatened each other, but they knew when to stop.

There were some people, though, who didn't respect anything. They'd sell their mother for a bottle of beer. Drunkards, half-wits and good-for-nothings, like you've got in every town. They didn't think twice about denouncing everybody. We found out afterward they got ten dollars for every deserter who was captured.

Take Ti-noir Côté and the others at the Restaurant Central. They had to answer to Courchesne the notary and Léger Crochetière, the Chief of Police. You'd always see a couple of them prowling around the notary's or the police station—when four or five weren't sitting around a table at the restaurant, plotting something.

They'd all had dealings with the Chief at one time or another. Léger Crochetière was a tremendously strong man. His voice was loud enough to stop most fights without even having to use his fists. He was the dictator of Nicolet and the surroundings.

Chief Crochetière abhorred the deserters. He hated each of them personally, even the ones he'd never met. He went after the ones he knew, of course, but he was just as interested in finding out about the deserters he didn't know.

He was in league with all the small-time criminals you can always find in the country.

"Now listen here, Ti-Clin! You do your patriotic duty and I'll forget that business at the Restaurant Traversy!"

Doing your patriotic duty meant only one thing: denouncing deserters. Besides, they all more or less owed their exemptions to Courchesne the notary and the Chief. That made them extra diligent!

For the deserters, it was a lot more dangerous to deal with Chief Crochetière than with the soldiers. Just think about it: the Chief knew the countryside inside out and was up on so many things that he held almost everybody in the palm of his hand. And then there was that money of his he'd been lending out left and right for the last twenty years.

That's how, from the fall of 1917 to, say, the beginning of

74

1919, he must have been responsible for arresting a good twenty deserters. And he picked up at least half of them himself.

At the start he alerted the military authorities as soon as he was fairly sure he'd discovered a deserter's hiding-place. But the soldiers quickly realized their little country excursions could be more deadly than they thought. The cowards they were hunting down like rabbits had guns and they knew how to use them. Some were determined to kill rather than be captured. And a soldier's body in the snowy forest, with the wolves and foxes— there wouldn't be much left come spring.

That's why the soldiers were satisfied to reconnoitre around the edges of the woods, without ever setting foot inside. In the evening, they'd report to their superiors and to Chief Crochetière, saying they'd gone through the forest with a fine-toothed comb. But no luck, they hadn't found anything.

Then Léger Crochetière would get angry. "I'll go get your damn wildcat for you!"

Next day, or two days later at the most, a deserter would be locked up in the Nicolet jail where the soldiers would come get him to take him to Montreal. They used to say back then that a man who'd refused to obey and was captured would spend a long time regretting he hadn't gone to war like everybody else.

That's why the deserters never stayed too long in the same hide-out. They had to find other places than the ones they'd normally think of first. The sugar shacks, for example, deep in the woods at the end of somebody's property, weren't safe any more.

Then winter set in with a vengeance. First a little white frost, then all the puddles froze over. Finally the earth got as hard as a rock. The wind blew bitterly cold. Then one night, the snow covered everything over at once.

The snow made martyrs of the deserters. They couldn't hunt, they couldn't trap, they couldn't even leave their hiding-places and take a step outside because they would have left footprints in the snow. They were condemned to their own prison.

For provisions, they had to count on a safe person who

knew their hide-outs and could come to them on stormy nights, when the fresh snow would cover their snowshoe tracks.

It was late November, early December. Nazaire was somewhere in that whiteness, with the blizzards and the Northern lights.

When you leave Nicolet for Sorel or Montreal, you take a little winding road along the Saint Lawrence that follows the river, though you don't see it. The road has been laid out to run from house to house, and they were built away from the river to shelter them from the terrible spring floods.

Between Nicolet and Sorel, you cross three rivers and you know their water will swell the Saint Lawrence, but you still can't see it. Just before Pierreville, the road curves twice and wanders farther from the water. At the first curve, a little path continues straight ahead. You take that one. If you follow it to the end, you reach the Saint-François River. And if you turn right and go alongside it, right away it's another world.

It's the realm of water. The village was built on both sides of the river. You see nothing but willows, unpainted board houses and wooden docks lashed to long poles. Boats too, with old brown sails and short stumpy masts.

A lot of people say it's the most picturesque village they've ever seen. You can see round nets stretched out between poles. There used to be children in blood-stained white smocks, busy "fixing" live perch on the docks. They'd stick their left hand in the bucket, grab a big fish, then clack! cut off the head, rip! gut it, two strokes and the skin is gone, clack! the tail and the job's done. They'd throw the head, the skin and the guts, still wriggling, into the water. Dozens of tame ducks swoop down on the remains. It goes on all afternoon.

A man who'd been through the village wouldn't soon forget it, but he'd leave without seeing the most important part if he didn't keep walking along the river another hour or so. There, in the vast marches, he'd see plots of farmland and big mowers at anchor right in the middle of the meadows. On one side is the river, on the other the marshy fields; you're never sure where the water begins and the earth ends.

And if you take a few more steps along the river, right away you come to hardened clay. The spring floods have stripped the willows as high as a man stands. Huge ferns grow there. Then there are rushes, water weeds and the ground gets softer and softer. It's harder and harder to walk on it. In the best places, you can see duck blinds made from cedar branches that have mildewed since the last season.

Then suddenly there's water! Not the river, the sea! Lake Saint-Pierre, an inland sea, so wide you can't see the other shore. It's a widening of the Saint Lawrence, and the banks are so swampy that no one goes there but hunters in the fall.

That's where Nazaire and his brother Eugène found themselves early in the winter of 1917. Eugène had fled too, after he'd gotten his notice for the medical. He went directly to the house in Port Saint-François, arriving the very day Nazaire was going to leave. The two brothers decided to hide together.

It was done at night. A farmer named Levasseur from La Baie du Febvre agreed to take them in his wagon. Two armed deserters are enough to convince anybody. They were dropped off at the big curve before Pierreville. They must have walked almost two hours to get around the village of Notre Dame de Pierreville. The first lights of dawn were glowing in the houses. They got lost in the swamp but they finally found the river. The Saint-François was frozen; it was December and the river had started freezing in mid-October.

Nazaire and Eugène finally reached a spot where some land had been cleared during the summer. Branches, stumps and heaps of earth, clay and sand were thrown up on the river bank. The mound made a little rise twice the height of a man. They dug a hiding-place in it by pushing aside the stumps and reinforcing the ceiling with branches. It worked perfectly. By pulling more branches over the doorway, the hide-out looked like nothing more than heaped-up trash from the land clearing.

It was safer than any of the deserters' usual hiding-places.

Nazaire and Eugène had found the spot where they could hide till the end of time if they needed to: in the earth itself.

Then the great black misery of winter began, no light, no fire, clinging to each other to keep warm. They had stretched out a blanket on the ground, on the rough floor of branches and frozen earth. On the side opposite the entrance, they had each set their pack that served as a pillow at night and a cushion during the day. From the ceiling they had hung two pots, a little mirror and a picture of the Holy Virgin.

Their hiding-place wasn't high enough to let them stand up, but it was quite deep, so they moved around on all fours. On one of the side walls they had fastened different useful little objects, utensils, a knife, two tin cups and several little bags where they put the potatoes, turnips, cabbages and the big piece of salt pork they had brought. On the side of the opening, they had hung another blanket that took the place of a door and was good for keeping the smells, smoke and light inside. They had tallow candles, but they lit them as rarely as possible because they gave off an intolerable smell when they burned.

They spent most of their time clinging to one another to keep warm. It didn't take long for them to hate each other as much as they loved each other. They cried together. They wiped each other's noses gently, then they hit each other in the face with their fists. They hugged each other like madmen, and the next minute they were about to strangle each other. They were like a couple of young pups.

It was even more unbearable because they could hardly ever go outside. They would have left footprints in the snow, and during the day somebody might have seen them. They were condemned to going out only on stormy nights. And then they didn't dare stray far because they were afraid of getting lost in the blizzards that blurred the line between the frozen river and the marshes. When the storms raged, they walked circles around their hiding-place like condemned men. They waved their arms in the air and stamped their feet on the hardened snow to warm

78

up. They were like characters in a fiendish tale or ghosts that return only in the dead of winter.

They could spend three or four days without going out. But they still had their needs. They had desires, like all men. They wanted to do what makes a man a man. The more time passed, the stronger it grew. They put their hands in their pants, each on his own. They never touched each other.

But to tell the truth, they must not have been that miserable. They had enough to eat, they weren't too cold and there were two of them. But for them winter was like a night, a long, cold, black night that would never end.

That's why they began prowling around their hiding-place more often than they should have. A sudden icy rain had fallen, forming a thick crust on the snow, and that made it easier. The two brothers could walk on it without leaving footprints. They made forays closer and closer to the village. They wanted to steal a chicken but all the henhouses were locked and guarded; it was the middle of the war and winter too.

Then they tried to enter a lonely little house. It was the end of day, just at dusk. All they had to do was push in a windowpane whose glass had been replaced by a piece of cardboard. They went into the summer kitchen. That's usually a big room at the back of the house where people in the country spent a lot of time during the summer. They cook there because it's cooler, and also because otherwise the men would get the whole house dirty when they come back from the fields wearing their big boots. During the winter, the summer kitchen was usually used to store supplies. There wasn't any heat, of course. The room was frozen from mid-October to mid-April with no let-up. It was perfect for keeping meat.

Nazaire and Eugène slipped into the summer kitchen in a lonely little house. They found a burlap bag and were about to search the cupboards. But a voice rooted them to the spot.

"If you need something, you'd be better off asking for it!"

The voice really didn't have much nastiness in it. There was a woman, watching them from the kitchen window. Nazaire and Eugène backed toward the wall, their hands behind them to feel for the window where they'd come in. The woman opened the door. She was wearing a flowered dress and a scarf on her head. Just opening the door sent a blast of good warm air into the summer kitchen. Nazaire and Eugène didn't move; they took in the warmth one last time. And deep inside both of them wanted to talk to somebody, to be with somebody for a few precious moments.

As it turned out, the woman said, "Come in and warm yourselves. Don't be afraid, come in!"

The brothers followed her to the threshold but they didn't go any further. They stayed there—it was already too good. They didn't dare sit down by the big two-tiered stove. They looked like two *coureurs des bois* who'd forgotten what the inside of a house was like.

The woman had already settled in by the stove. She turned her grey head toward them. "Come and sit down," she said. "Come along! Don't be afraid! There's nothing to fear, I'm all alone in here. You haven't a thing to fear, I've seen my share of deserters. If you'd like to know, I've nothing against them. Come and sit down!"

And the two brothers' resistance melted like the snow from their boots on the floor. They edged closer like frightened dogs, and it took them quite a while before they sank all the way into the two rockers the woman had pulled next to hers in front of the stove. They listened to her talk without paying much attention to what she said, busy as they were getting reacquainted with the fire. They only listened with one ear, but they still managed to understand that this grey-haired woman in her fifties was the widow Landry, that she'd lost her husband one misty dawn on Lake Saint-Pierre and that she'd raised her sixteen children by herself. She'd just found a job for her youngest as a house-keeper for Father Nadeau in Saint-Elphège. Now she was alone in her little house on the outskirts of the village, with nothing but a sick old elm to watch over her.

"So you see," she said, "I'm all alone as well."

And the two brothers felt their trust growing as the heat thawed their blood. They began by taking off their fur caps, then they untied their *ceintures fléchées* and opened their grey coats. Finally, they pulled off their boots and put their feet, wrapped in brightly coloured heavy wool socks, on the open oven door.

They felt so trusting and had such a need to confide in somebody that Nazaire was about to say who they were and where they came from. But the widow interrupted them sharply.

"No offense intended," she said, "but I'd just as soon not know anything about you. You don't have to have a crystal ball to guess that you're a couple of good *Canadiens* and that you're not from around here. That's good enough for me. The less you know, the better it is! I don't need to know your names to practice Christian charity, like Our Lord Jesus Christ teaches us. You just wait there, I'll be back!"

She went to the corner of the kitchen where a cupboard was built into the wall. She pulled out a large, chipped white plate on which there was a generous piece of roast pork. Then she took a little brown pan in which there could be nothing else than the drippings from the roast, the good dark kind with white jelly on top. Some bread too: a big loaf, not even started. She put all of it on the corner of the table nearest the stove. It was like a feast on the old oilcloth.

Nazaire and Eugène ate greedily, forgetting the rules of politeness. All that was heard were the little noises they made as they gobbled down the food. Then the widow cleared the table and set a big basin of water in front of them, along with an old razor with a mother-of-pearl handle, some soap and a shaving brush with a few sparse hairs. The two brothers washed and shaved obediently.

"Now you look like real Christians!"

She wanted to have them sleep in the downstairs room. Eugène refused firmly.

"Don't be afraid," the widow insisted, "I stay up all night by the stove. At my age you don't sleep much any more. If ever I hear something I'll wake you up, but there's nothing to fear. Nobody ever comes by and everybody knows I live all alone."

But Eugène explained that if they slept one single night in a

81

good bed, they would never have the strength to go back where they came from. The widow said she understood and offered, in the course of a rambling conversation like you might have around the stove on a winter afternoon, to go from time to time to bring them a little coffee and hot food.

"No need to tell me exactly where you are. All we have to do is agree on a place, anywhere, where you can see me coming. And you can come pick up my basket once I've left."

But there was no formal agreement at the start. Nothing but yesses and heads nodding. Finally, all in one breath, the widow declared that Christmas was coming and that they couldn't go through the Holidays without the aid of religion.

"You're not animals," she said in a shocked voice. "I'll send you Father Nadeau. Whatever else, you can't doubt a priest's word! He has his share of deserters, Father Nadeau has! This is more or less his parish here, and from time to time he comes to bring my daughter. Trust him, he's a man of great kindness."

Finally, around nine o'clock at night, Nazaire explained where their hide-out was to widow Landry, and the two brothers set out in the squall, their caps pulled down to their eyes. But once they were back in their hole, they began to quarrel.

"You should never have told her where we were," Eugène grumbled. "We should never take risks. She might squeal on us!"

Nazaire took offense. There was nothing to fear from widow Landry. And he was right. Widow Landry had such a good heart that the idea of denouncing a deserter would have never occurred to her. In her mind, these boys were simply children who were a little more difficult than the rest. And difficult children, she knew a thing or two about them!

It was eleven o'clock one morning. The sun was glistening on the snow. One of those mornings when suddenly you hear the river ice cracking sharply in the cold, like a rifle shot. It was a little before Christmas.

Nazaire and Eugène were curled up in a ball at the bottom of their black hole. They were dozing but one of them was always responsible for lifting up the entryway blanket from time to time and taking a look through the gridwork of branches that formed the opening. Eugène crawled over to it, pushed aside the branches, then he turned to Nazaire, shook him violently and whispered harshly in his ear, "Somebody's coming! A man by himself wearing a wildcat coat!"

There was an uproar in the hide-out, a quick scuffling to put the battle preparations into action: push back the blankets, clear the space to manoeuvre more easily. Nazaire was responsible for taking up position by the opening. Eugène was to hide at the back and be ready in case Nazaire was hit.

Nazaire was ready to fire, his 12-gauge in his hand, his cap pushed up on his forehead. The man was coming closer, lifting his feet high in the snow; he looked as if he was searching for something. He halted a few steps from the entrance to the hide-out. He inspected the surroundings and bent over the ground—he was looking for footprints, for sure. The man straightened up, took three steps and put his hand on the branches that hid the opening to the hide-out. Just as he was about to push them aside, the mean-looking barrel of a hunting rifle came out slowly and pressed against his chest.

"Friend," said the man, "don't shoot! I am Father Nadeau from Saint-Elphège."

"Stay where you are," Nazaire replied. "Don't move!"

He kept his eye on him through the branches. But the man began untying his *ceinture fléchée* that was wound around his wildcat coat three times. He opened it up.

"See my cassock!"

"That doesn't prove anything," Nazaire answered. "Show me your hands!"

The man took off his big leather mittens. His hands were white, true enough, even if they were big and short. He might have been a priest, but his father was a farmer.

"No offense intended, Father," said Nazaire, "I'm going to ask you to say something in Latin."

The man smiled and began reciting some Vobiscums, Te Deums, Absolvo Tes and all sorts of Latin phrases that the most Christian of French Canadians wouldn't understand, though he'd heard them a thousand times at church. No doubt about it, nobody but a priest could talk like that!

Then Nazaire let Father Nadeau from Saint-Elphège crawl into the hide-out next to him. He introduced his brother Eugène to him, but Eugène was in a very bad mood and answered the visitor's questions with a grunt.

So Nazaire and Father Nadeau talked to each other, squatting face to face. The priest had blessed the place when he came in and Nazaire had been eager to point out his picture of the Holy Virgin. But first the conversation had been about the everyday concerns of life. Father Nadeau wanted to know if the two brothers had enough to eat, if they weren't too cold and unhappy too often. Then his comments skillfully turned to spiritual matters: he wanted to know if, every morning, the two unfortunate young men weren't forgetting to consecrate their day to the Lord.

"How do you expect us to?" Eugène retorted. "In here there's no difference between day and night! It's all the same."

Father Nadeau pretended not to hear the disobliging remark. He moved onto the approaching Nativity, emphasizing the sacred character of the holiday and reminding them that, to redeem all those who were suffering, the Saviour had wanted to be born in a stable. He pointed out that the manger in Bethlehem was very similar to the two men's hide-out, and Eugène muttered that it was a lot worse here because it was a cold country and there wasn't even any straw. But the priest didn't hear. He announced he was going to hear their confessions. Nazaire and Eugène each went out while the other entrusted his sins to the priest, then Father Nadeau celebrated mass right there in their hiding-place, on a little white cloth he had brought on which he precariously balanced his portable crucifix for last rites and a little altar stone containing precious relics. The two brothers and Father Nadeau were squatting together. All three of them were murmuring the Latin words, and at the moment of the elevation, the big wildcat coat slipped from the priest's shoulders. He went on with his ceremony as if nothing had happened. And every time Nazaire and Eugène opened their mouths to pronounce the responses of the Mass, a little white cloud rose up like incense.

After the ceremony, the priest conversed with them for a good hour. They spoke of Nicolet, where he'd gone to the *Grand Séminaire*. Nazaire and Eugène remembered their lives before the events, and so they came to recall their acts. Father Nadeau said that the Good Lord could not turn his wrath against people who disobeyed unjust commandments to escape killing their fellow men.

"Thou shalt not kill!" he pronounced solemnly, "is the greatest of all the commandments."

Then Father Nadeau felt obliged to explain his position. He might have put it diffcrently than the other priests, that was true, but several of them, so he said, all thought the same way. Personally, he felt no shame exercising his ministry to deserters. In fact, he considered it his duty, and his conscience drove him to watch over their physical well-being as well as the salvation of their souls.

"A human being can't remain hidden away for months without seeing anybody," he said. "He must fraternize with his fellow men to retain his sense of values and his respect for society. Otherwise, he'll be like an animal by the time he comes out. That's why I'm offering to take you to Saint-Elphège, one at a time, to spend the evening with some people I know who are completely trustworthy."

The two brothers stared at each other in astonishment. That was certainly the last offer they would have expected. They'd gotten used to the idea that they'd have to stay hidden until the end of the war, and even a little longer, and here somebody was inviting them into their homes!

"We can't accept," Eugène answered quickly. "It's too dangerous."

"No, it's not!" replied Father Nadeau. "I know what I'm doing; you can trust me. If it was too dangerous I wouldn't offer

85

to do it. I'll take you to a farmer's house on the sixth concession in Saint-Elphège. He's a fine man even if he does have a coarse tongue. He's not rich but he has a good heart. He has six children and his wife is an excellent house-keeper."

The two brothers faced each other, each with his own opinion. Eugène seemed locked into his determination to refuse the offer but Nazaire was tempted.

"Are you sure it's not too dangerous?" he asked.

"There's nothing to fear. I'll take one of you with me in my wagon at dusk. If ever anybody questions us, I'll say I'm on my way to bring the Holy Sacrament to an elderly person, and that wouldn't even be a lie because as it turns out I plan to stop at old lady Brochu's house on the way back. And if anybody asks me who's sitting next to me, I'll say he's my altarboy. There's nothing untrue about that either. Don't worry! I've done this plenty of times and I know the Good Lord will be with us."

A few moments later, the two brothers were quarrelling in front of the priest. Eugène wouldn't hear of it. He grabbed Nazaire by the collar. On all fours, facing each other, they'd knocked over the little bottle of holy water the priest had left on the cloth that he'd used as an altar.

"Are you crazy?" Eugène repeated. "You know it makes no sense! We said we'd stick together until the end! I'm warning you, if you go, you won't find me here when you get back."

Father Nadeau tried to make Eugène listen to reason.

"But don't you see, it's for your own good! Look, you're already behaving like savages!"

"You let us settle this ourselves!"

But Nazaire had turned a deaf ear to him. He didn't want to hurt his brother Eugène, but he couldn't help wanting to spend a warm evening in the kitchen of a real house, especially before the Holidays. Already he pictured the children around the table, their hands folded behind their backs. He heard them

86

singing the only hymn you're permitted to sing during Advent:

Venez, Divin Messie,
Sauver nos jours infortunés!
Vous êtes notre vie!
Venez, venez, venez!

They might only eat boiled potatoes, certainly no meat, let alone a dessert! It was Advent, people were preparing for the celebration. Nazaire couldn't bear it any more. Hastily he gathered his knife, his rosary—mostly to please Father Nadeau —his big clean handkerchief and the little coil of rope he used to take everywhere he went.

Eugène repeated, "I'm warning you, you won't find me here when you get back!"

But Nazaire didn't hear him. He kissed him tenderly and followed Father Nadeau out into the blue air. The two men headed toward the village of Notre-Dame. At widow Landry's house they met up with Françoise, the young house-keeper visiting her mother. Hastily the priest hitched up the sleigh and the three of them sat down side by side on the bench, the runners whistling on the icy road, by the glow of a low twilight that foretold snow for the night.

The two men had seated Françoise between them and covered their legs with a big brown caribou skin that smelled of horses. Nazaire swung his hefty arm around the back of the bench and when they took a curve, he hung on with all his might, which made him lean against the girl's shoulder. The clouds raced above them. Nazaire was touched and between his clenched teeth he sang, *Venez, Divin Messie!*

The horse seemed to know the way. Nazaire couldn't have said how long they'd glided over the icy road before they spotted the lights of a village. It was the first one they'd ridden through after they'd dropped off Françoise at the presbytery: fifty houses around a meager looking wooden church.

They slipped through the night a while longer, then Father Nadeau pulled on the reins.

"Whoa! We're here! Whoa, grey mare!"

The sleigh came to a halt in the yard of a lonely farm. There was more light from the stable than from the windows of the house. A little man came out, wearing a red and black checked shirt, his hands bare and his head covered with a brightly coloured cap.

In the cold air, he shouted, "Christ on a crutch! It must be the devil himself coming to roust us out this time of night. Who could the damned old trickster have sent us this time, for the bloody love of Jesus?"

He came closer, waving his hands in the air. As soon as he recognized Father Nadeau, he respectfully removed his cap.

"My deepest apologies, Father. I didn't recognize you."

"No harm done, Auguste, no harm done to me, but you could at least let the Good Lord's name alone during Advent."

"It's bigger than me, Father. I inherited it from my late father."

"I know, Auguste, I know! But look who I brought with me."

And with his big mitten he pointed to Nazaire who was wrapped up in the caribou skin.

"A poor young man," the priest went on, "a good fellow who's fallen on hard times lately."

"You'll get over it!" the man said in his frightening voice. "You're not going to spend the evening freezing yourselves out here in the yard, are you? I bet you haven't eaten anything!"

And he turned toward the stable; two figures were standing in the low doorway. "Hey, in there! Baptiste! Arthur! Come and unhitch Father Nadeau's horse!"

And he led them promptly into the overheated kitchen where a blast of icy air swept in at the same time they did. The mother and two of her daughters were standing by the big wood stove. A bony dog came up to sniff them with a growl, then went back to lie under the stove. The chairs were already pulled out.

"Come and get warm, Christ on a bike!"

Nazaire tried not to stick out too much. He sat down as far away as possible, in the darkest corner of the kitchen.

"This young man has had a hard life just lately," the priest explained, pointing to Nazaire. "You can be sure that where he's living, he doesn't see many people. That's why I decided to bring him to spend the evening. He's a fine fellow, I guarantee it."

Nazaire smiled. "Good evening, everybody," he said.

And turning to the priest, he said, "The Good Lord is certainly merciful to have allowed me to meet you."

"You'll get over it!" the man thundered.

A moment of silence. The mother and her daughters busied themselves around the stove. The door opened and the two from the stable came in, two boys of fifteen or sixteen with thin mustaches and pipes in their mouths.

They ate in silence after having recited the Benedicite standing up, with big signs of the cross. From time to time the father thundered, "Arthur, bread! More potatoes, Elise!"

After supper everybody filled his pipe, including the priest, and Nazaire lay low in his corner. The lamp lit the deserted table.

Finally, Nazaire said, "We'd better start thinking of going. It's late already."

But the priest motioned him to stay put. So Nazaire sunk down a little further into his chair and from under his thick eyebrows, he watched the people passing the evening. The father and his two sons were smoking. The mother and her daughters were around the table, darning multi-coloured socks and lumberjack shirts. And the priest talked in his droning voice. He talked about how Christmas was coming up and about the uncertain times they were living in. Around nine-thirty, Auguste went out to have a look in the stable, and he came back with the news that big snowflakes had started to fall.

"Would you like to stay the night?" the mother asked. "It would be such an honour for us!"

"I have to be going," the priest answered, "but without abusing your kindness, I'd like to ask you to keep my young friend for the night. He'll be better off here than in the village and besides, it will do him good to be with a family for a night."

Nazaire tried to protest but he was drowned out in a flood of gestures and words. Then Father Nadeau left, saying he'd return to pick up Nazaire the next morning. A half hour later, Nazaire was stretched out on the beggar's bench next to the stove. Everything around him was dark and the reflection of the fire that slipped through the chinks in the stove door made will-o-the-wisps on his blanket.

He lay on his back, unable to sleep. And he couldn't help wondering how he would escape if somebody came knocking on the door. To calm himself, he began reviewing the faces of the evening. Without realizing it, his mind came to rest on the face of the oldest daughter, Elise.

Now that he was back all alone in his hole again, Nazaire shivered like a drowned rat. Sitting hunched over, he rocked back and forth all day. The last days of December were turning out to be colder than usual. And Nazaire had only his frozen breath to keep him company.

He dozed on and off all day, like a puppy, an hour or two at a time, never more. He would have easily lost track of time if he hadn't been especially careful to keep the big pocket watch running that Father Nadeau had given him. With his knife he made cuts on a branch that served as a calendar, and so he made his way, hour by hour, toward the miraculous moment of Christmas when, it seemed to him, a great miracle might come to pass.

At night, he pushed aside the opening of his hiding-place to examine the stars, trying to reckon which of these points of light might have guided the Three Wise Men to Bethlehem. That had happened long ago; perhaps the star had gone out in the meantime. Besides, those things had taken place in such distant lands!

The most pessimistic thoughts began to assail him. Perhaps this Christmas would mark the passage of the exterminating angel. Perhaps the end of the world would find him huddled in his hiding-place, frozen to death. Nazaire remembered having heard of those missionaries of the Far North, white fathers with prophet's beards, who had lain down by their wolf dogs on the frozen tundra, never to wake again. Shivers ran down his spine. That's why, in spite of all caution, he began to sing the exhalting hymns of Christmas at the top of his lungs, day and night.

"*Glo-ooooo-ooooo-ooooo-ria! In excelsis Deo!*"

Night and day merged. The wind buffeted the frozen Saint-François River; the stars, paralyzed by the cold, hovered on the horizon an extra measure longer. Then the snow brought milder weather. For hours, flakes as big as a fist fell. The silence thickened. Then the cold took hold of the air with a single blast. Snow began to fall in dense little pellets. Day and night.

And with his pocket knife, Nazaire began whittling the little branches that pushed through the walls of his hiding-place. First a little Baby Jesus, as big as a finger, with a little round head, lying on some wisps of straw. A Holy Virgin carved into a curved branch, better to bend over the infant. A St. Joseph with a bark beard. Three or four shepherds rising from the edges and sheep everywhere, barely sketched into the ends of the branches.

Sometimes Nazaire lit his candle to guide the Wise Men. Not too long because of the smell, but just enough to show the way. For he had not the slightest doubt that the Three Wise Men had set out on their journey, somewhere across Lake Saint-Pierre, frozen and snow-covered like a desert. They were heading toward the humble manger and Nazaire was sure there couldn't be a manger anywhere as humble as his.

And on the evening of the twenty-fourth of December, just at midnight, on his knees before his sculpted branches, the deserter intoned *Minuit, chrétiens*:

> *Minuit, chrétiens, c'est l'heure solennelle*
> *Où l'homme-Dieu descendit jusqu'à nous*
> *Pour effacer la tache originelle*
> *Et de son Père apaiser le courroux.*

Warmth filled him at the same time as the smell of the steaming *tourtières* and the plump turkey. His father was standing in the centre of the room, hands crossed before him. He was saying, "The Baby Jesus was born this night to save mankind. He was born for the poor and the unfortunate, for those who are hungry and cold. For Nazaire and for Eugène, our children whom we haven't heard from. For all the boys of Nicolet too who went to war and who are shivering this night at the bottom of their trenches."

Then he blessed the family kneeling at the foot of the tree. Nazaire fell into a deep sleep.

The snow had fallen thicker than usual that winter. By the end of January, Nazaire hadn't been able to take a step outside for two long weeks. Still the same thing: a single footprint in the snow could have given him away. Besides condemning him to reclusion, it created a rather delicate problem: waste.

For cooking, it was easy enough, he just had to push his potato peelings between the branches, but his human waste was more serious. Widow Landry had given him an old bucket. He took care of his needs in it, but how could he get rid of its contents? It stank. He pushed the bucket as far away as possible and tried not to think about it.

Nazaire spent long hours rolled up in a ball, contemplating a picture he had preciously stored in his memory, one that was mingled at times with that of the Virgin of the Christmas celebration: Elise's face. He saw her again two or three times in February. Father Nadeau arrived at the end of the day when it was beginning to snow, and he took Nazaire in his sleigh toward Saint-Elphège.

"I wouldn't put a dog outside in this weather," Cormier the farmer said. "But that's just the time you two go out. One fine day we'll find you frozen stiff in the snow, with your sleigh tipped over. Not very Christian."

Father Nadeau smiled and Nazaire stood in his corner, soaking up the warmth and the presence of Elise who was busy in the kitchen. He was practically purring with pleasure and he went as far as forgetting the war, his hole and fear itself. One day, however, Father Nadeau set out the events clearly before him.

On the big table at the Cormiers' house, he opened *La*

Presse and began reading out loud. In Quebec City, on the evening of the twenty-ninth of March, five soldiers arrested a man named Mercier in a poolroom. He didn't have his exemption papers on him. That was just at a time when the people in Quebec City, like those in Montreal and Shawinigan, were getting tired of the Army's provocations. People were openly saying that the soldiers were arresting young men and tearing up their exemption papers right in front of them to recruit them forcibly. Then what had to happen happened. On Easter Monday, the first of April, the wife of a man named Honoré Bergeron became worried about her husband's absence. She crossed the city where the riots had been raging for three days to discover her husband was in the military prison. She went in search of him; she was to find him only that night, at the Hubert-Moisan Morgue. Another widow who didn't know it yet, young Madame Alexandre Bussières, had to go to the Moisan Morgue to see her husband again. Shortly after the proclamation of the Riot Act, the soldiers were heard to shout threats like, "Now you goddamn sons of bitches will do your duty!" But hadn't the Riot Act been read in English only, to demonstrators who hadn't understood a single word of it? That, at least, was what several witnesses confirmed.

It was at the corner of Saint-Vallier and Bagot, in Quebec City. It must have been between eleven and eleven-thirty at night. Who had given the order to the soldiers to fire? There were four or five hundred of them. Who had given them the order to fire? In any case, the wounds had been inflicted by a machine gun; the doctors who examined the dead and the wounded confirmed it. The people had also fired on the soldiers. Some soldiers had been wounded in the legs, one in the jaw. "This one is dead!" one of the Army commanders said to Father Evans, pointing to a man named Demers. And the priest kneeled down in the street to pray for the repose of his soul. The soldiers turned to him. "Get out of here! You have no business here! We have orders to fire at everyone!"

The two other riot victims were named Tremblay and Desmeules. Both were hit by explosive bullets. Bullets like for big game hunting! Bullets that are forbidden to be used, even in war! Another man, Ovide Blouin, had to have his leg amputated. All the bones were shattered.

There were, so they say, children on top of snowbanks, throwing icicles and singing *O Canada* and *La Marseillaise*. They were shouting, "We're *Canadiens* and we're no cowards!" Witnesses heard the soldiers answer them in English, "You French bastards!"

In the end, everybody knew that the responsibility for the riots could be laid at the door of the "spotters." The spotters were informers recruited from among the shadiest of the French Canadians. They squealed on the men who didn't have their exemption papers. A lawyer had certified that four of his clients had had their exemption certificates torn up by the spotters. That was the attitude of the group that had provoked the riots. The people wanted to take out their anger on the Army offices where the spotters were recruited and where some of them had taken refuge. The mayor of Quebec City had refused to give the order to fire to the garrison. He'd said, You can rebuild a building, but not a man! But two days later the Army had opened fire. Sure, they'd read the Riot Act—but in English! And nobody had heard it. And the Army had opened fire with machine guns and explosive bullets, in the streets of Quebec City!

There were four killed, numerous wounded and fifty-eight arrested. Nazaire and the others couldn't get over it. War in the streets of Quebec City! They sat in silence around the table in Cormier the farmer's house.

Finally, Father Nadeau said, "Violence always leads to violence. Let us pray for those who died and ask the Lord that we country people be spared these trials."

Everybody kneeled and said the rosary, during which the sorrowful mysteries were evoked, it goes without saying. Then Nazaire took his spot on the beggar's bench. He had trouble falling asleep; images of the riots haunted him. To calm himself, once again he turned to the gentle face of Elise Cormier. For without realizing it, Nazaire treasured her already, even if the two of them hadn't spoken ten sentences to each other since they'd first met.

Nazaire was very happy to be back in his hiding-place. The story of the events in Quebec City had moved him to resolve not to go out until the war was good and over—not a minute before. He bore his cross patiently, you might say. He wrapped himself up as best he could and kept repeating, I'd rather freeze all alone in this hole than deal with the soldiers. I'll wait twenty years if I have to!

Besides, it was warming up. The beginning of April had arrived, and some afternoons Nazaire plucked up the courage to push back the entryway blanket and let in a little of the sun that was beginning to warm up. The snow was melting away from underneath. There were big purple patches in the fields that showed there was water below.

It was a Thursday, at nightfall. The river ice had suddenly covered over with water. Large streams were forming on top. Nazaire was beginning to get worried. He knew that the break-up could bring floods that would crest as fast as a galloping horse. And as far as he could tell, if there was a major flood, his hole would be swamped right away.

He was hesitating when the first loud cracking noises were heard from across the way, on the other side of the river. It was dark now, and Nazaire couldn't see a thing. In his memory he pictured the terrible break-ups of the Nicolet River that brought the water right to the back of his parents' house.

He didn't know the Saint-François very well, but when he thought about it, this river must behave more or less the same as the Nicolet. The ice from upstream would begin to "walk" under the force of the run-off, and all this shattered ice would jam under the unbroken surface of the river mouth. That would definitely bring on a flood that could last a day or two.

Nazaire was at the point of deciding that it might be better to run when, in the distance, on the Notre-Dame side, he heard a powerful rumbling. The river had begun to move. Hastily,

95

Nazaire gathered up a blanket, some provisions and the little prayerbook that Father Nadeau had given him. He began walking quickly toward the village, then he broke into a run. Stealthily, the water was spreading everywhere; already it must have invaded the hiding-place where he had just spent the winter. He turned around and stared for a moment into the darkness before him, then he continued walking at a good clip toward widow Landry's house.

Now they were sitting in front of the stove, he and the widow, listening to the time pass and telling each other, with long silences, about the break-ups and storms they had known. Dawn was beginning to sketch out the shape of the windows. A gentle complicity had grown between the two of them. In the morning it was agreed that Nazaire would move into the attic.

In the days that followed, he was able to see just how much the winter months had shaken him. He was prey to sudden fears, uncontrollable terrors. He shut himself up in a troubling silence. The widow brought him up a nice big bowl of pea soup and he didn't say a word. Sometimes she even found him sitting on the floor in a corner like a sulking child. He remained motionless for hours, as if he'd lost all connection with life.

The widow managed to find different pretexts to go up to the attic several times a day. Changing a blanket, putting sheets on the straw mattress, bringing little cakes she'd just taken out of the oven. She fussed over Nazaire as if he was a sickly little child. She always wore her big blue shawl over her shoulders. She sat down by him, took his hand and said, "You should come down once in a while to the kitchen, my boy. It will do you good."

Nazaire answered with an absent look, "That's not where I belong. Deserters have no business in houses. In the attic is good enough!"

"But don't you see," the widow insisted. "Don't you see I only want the best for you?"

In his daydreams, in the deepest moments of his solitude, Nazaire had even begun to suspect that widow Landry and Father Nadeau had leagued together to squeal on him to the spotters for ten dollars.

"You see," said the widow, "since your mama isn't here, it's a little like I'm taking her place."

And she took his head and rocked him tenderly against her breast like a child. Nazaire whimpered softly.

"I don't want anybody to love me! I'm like a dead person, like I was dead, you understand! I'm all alone over here, with the dead people. I see you, I hear you, but I can't talk to you. I'm like a ghost!"

"Don't talk like that," the widow said, rocking him. "The war will end, you'll see, and then afterwards everything will be like before."

"I'll never be like before. Never!"

"That's true," the widow answered. "You'll never be exactly like before. But that's for the better. Before you were still a boy, and when you leave here you'll be a man, a real man!"

"If that's what a man is!" Nazaire grumbled.

And the widow pressed his head against her big flowered apron. Like a lullaby she repeated, "Those are all just silly ideas in your head. You're talking like that because you're tired. They've got to finish up their war as fast as they can so you can leave here! I'm not the one to keep you company. I'm doing my best, but I'm an old lady! What you need is a woman, one your own age! A woman of your own. With children too. You'll come home in the evening, and there'll be your wife and your children ... "

Sometimes Nazaire fell asleep in the widow's arms.

Three days later there was a knock on the widow's door. She was busy putting wood in the stove. She turned around and spotted two soldiers through the window of the kitchen door.

It was the end of April; the soldiers had returned with the good weather. These two really did look relaxed, smiling even, with their caps on the sides of their heads.

The widow ran to her room and banged the broom handle on the ceiling as they'd agreed on to let Nazaire know not to make a sound. Then she went to open the door very slowly.

"Madame," said one of the soldiers. "We have to requisition your horse."

"What horse? I don't have a horse!"

"We must have the wrong information."

"But what do you want a horse for?"

"To patrol the marshes along the river."

"You'd be better off taking a boat if you want to go over there!"

"Is the water high?"

"*Monsieur*, the water is as high as a horse's head. You'd be better off waiting until after the May tides!"

And the soldiers went away just as they'd come. But they had made it clear they were back, and they would be returning. The first thing the widow did was have Father Nadeau alerted, and during the night he took Nazaire to the Cormiers' farm on the sixth concession.

"Christ on a crutch!" Cormier the farmer said. "If that isn't the limit! Running after fellows who did nothing instead of going to war! But they'll have to get up early if they want to find you here, my boy! Anyway, they already came about a week ago. I sent them off to sniff their boots, *Calvaire!*"

And Nazaire followed Cormier the farmer into the barn. They toiled there all morning in their shirt sleeves, in the good smell of the hay. With the help of their pitchforks, they moved a big pile of hay to near the centre of the barn. They shored up a long corridor, then an entire room.

Finally, they amply covered over the whole construction.

"You'll have sweet dreams in there," Cormier the farmer said with a laugh. "Christ on a crutch! I'm starting to envy your fate!"

And Nazaire took possession of his kingdom. He imagined one bale of hay as an armchair, another as a couch. The floor was completely covered with hay too, so he had his choice of beds to sleep in. There was a pitcher for water, and one piece of wooden furniture: a little table made from a butter crate, but no lamp. No lamp nor candle nor pipe. No open flame! During the day Nazaire crept up to the entrance of the corridor and made

98

himself a little opening through which he could just make out the light from a high gable window criss-crossed with spider webs. He was warm enough and the smell was pleasant.

Three times a day they brought him his meals. And he who'd lost the habit of eating well waited impatiently for meal-time in hopes of seeing Elise's sweet face, at least half the time. Their conversations were never very elaborate.

"Good day, *mademoiselle* Elise!"

"Good day to you, *monsieur* Nazaire!"

"What's the weather like today?"

"The sun is out. The snow is all melted now. A little brisk but nice all the same."

"And how about you? What are you doing?"

"What am *I* doing? Oh, nothing special, you can be sure of that. I'm helping my mother in the kitchen.

"Did you make this?"

'Yes, I did. Now eat, it'll get cold."

That was the extent of their conversations in the first days of the month of May, 1918. Little by little, the danger passed, and they let Nazaire in to sit with them.

"Come on in, Christ on a crutch!" thundered Cormier the farmer. "Don't stay in the corner like that. Come and sit down!"

And Nazaire was growing more and more at ease. He smiled at everybody and did his best to say intelligent things. He spoke softly, but with confidence. He held his cap in his hand and smoked the pipe Cormier had given him to replace the one he'd lost in the break-up.

And some evenings, Nazaire suddenly felt in the mood to take a seat not too far from *mademoiselle* Elise. Then, becoming embarrassed, he didn't say a word the entire evening. The Cormier parents noticed this routine but they didn't pay much attention to it. After all, a man you're hiding like that in your hay can't be all bad.

Nazaire spent long hours during the day amusing himself by making Elise's face appear and disappear in his mind's eye. And the girl's ringlets filled the deserter's heart with a gentle warmth.

One morning, around eleven, a cart entered the yard, the horse in a lather. An ugly, poorly dressed little man jumped down and ran to the barn. Nazaire hit the dirt. Cormier the farmer was there, busy preparing the litter to carry to the stable. The little man asked him right off, "Are you Cormier?"

"Yes, and what about you?"

"Lalancette, Ephrem, from Notre-Dame de Pierreville, down the way. Widow Landry sent me. She said, Go to Mr. Cormier's house on the sixth concession in Saint Elphège and don't stop on the way. Tell him this to the letter: The war isn't over. The soldiers came back. Take your precautions. I don't understand what that means exactly," the little man went on, "but I swear to you that's what she said."

"Go on, Christ on a crutch!"

"Go on, go on ... I don't know which way to start! This is how it happened. The widow didn't ask me to tell you this, it's me who's talking now. There I was in my field with my horse. It's down the way, in the bottomland, by the Lake. I was just about to start harrowing. But before harrowing, in my field, you have to pick up all the wood that's dropped there every spring by the flood waters. There's so much water where we are, *Monsieur*, that even at this very moment I stand before you, there's still parts of my land under water. So I was in my field. I was picking up the wood and the piles of rushes. I hear steps in back of me. I'm surprised because usually you're left alone all day with just the horse to keep you company. I turn around. There's half a dozen soldiers, all dressed up in khaki. Some of them are even talking English. The biggest one—that must have been the commander—asks me for my papers, in French. I didn't have them on me. I never carry them, I'm too afraid of losing them. And who do you think is going to ask me for them? My horse? I didn't have them. But I'd heard talk that anybody who was captured without their papers could be taken into the Army, right away, just like that, without having a thing to say about it. I started running, then and there. The commander started shouting after me, Stop or we'll shoot! Then I understood it was serious. I stopped. They searched me. They escorted me to my house. I showed them my papers. The commander gave me a funny look and said to me, It was very dangerous, what you did. You could have been killed."

"Christ on a crutch!" Cormier the farmer said. "Come in, I'll give you something to drink."

"I won't say no!"

The little *caribou* glasses were on the oilcloth. The mother and her daughters were darning socks. The little man from Notre-Dame rolled himself a cigarette and he talked as he lit it. He explained that the soldiers had received orders to bring in all the deserters. They'd spent a week over by Pierreville, Saint-François du Lac and Notre-Dame de Pierreville. They'd searched everywhere, they'd more or less fired at everything that moved, they'd done so much damage it was as if there'd been a little war in the area. To sum it up, there were four deserters captured, one killed and two wounded.

As you might expect, as soon as Ephrem Lalancette left, the farmer ran to the barn. If you'd followed him inside, you would have thought he was talking to himself. He paced back and forth in front of the haystack.

"It's not over, Christ on a crutch, it's not over! Lay low, my boy! Not a word, not a move! Or else you're finished for good! There's soldiers everywhere! *Maudite race de Calvaire!* They killed one, that's what they say. One of our boys!"

He paced back and forth in front of the haystack, scratching his head and waving his arms in the air.

"You'd think they want to keep us from doing our harvesting like everybody else! Who's going to give us a hand this summer if our best young fellows still have to be hiding? Who's going to do it? In any case, my boy, no use thinking about coming in to sit with us these days! Don't take a step out of there, I'm telling you! Lie low! Understand?"

And a voice from beyond the tomb made itself heard.

"If this keeps up I'm going to die in here. It's darker than the devil's place and I'm running out of air."

"Better to run out of air little by little," answered Cormier, "than to run out all at once, Christ on a crutch!"

And the heavy silence of the country fell over the barn once more. A silence so pure it was cutting. With, from time to time, deep swells of sound: buckets being rinsed in the stable or a cow complaining because she's about to calve.

It was eleven-thirty. People eat early in the country. Elise had gone to the barn to bring Nazaire's dinner. She came back an instant later in tears, the full platter in her hands.

"Spit it out, Christ on a crutch! Is he dead? Spit it out!"

"I looked everywhere. I couldn't find him."

"How about that? He couldn't have disappeared into thin air like a puff of smoke!"

"Come and look! I'm telling you there's nobody there!"

And the whole family dropped whatever they were doing then and there—the kettle half-open, the pitchfork stuck in the ground, the dishes on the table—to rush to the barn. Nobody! Empty! The tunnel in the hay, the cavern in the hay, empty! No more blanket or water pitcher or kitchen utensils or bucket for his needs! Nothing but an odour. Nazaire couldn't have been gone for long.

The two boys ran from one end of the barn to the other, they climbed into the hayloft, they went to the stable and they came back. Nothing. Cormier the farmer scratched his head under his cap and muttered a few Christ on a crutches. The three women were whimpering together into their shawls.

"What could have happened to him? Didn't you others hear anything? You were outside, weren't you? It's a damn shame being deaf at your age!"

The two boys talked at the same time to try to explain what had happened.

"Go help Caillette have her calf. I don't want to see your faces, Christ on a crutch!"

And Cormier the farmer chased them away with a few waves of his cap.

The three women had sought refuge in the kitchen, in the smell of the soup. Elise was crumpling her apron in her hands.

102

"What could have happened?"

"Maybe somebody came and we didn't notice it!"

"We would have heard! We didn't hear anything!"

"Maybe he went away by himself."

"He could have told us!"

"Maybe he didn't have the time. Maybe something happened."

"Where could he have gone?"

"He doesn't know anybody around here besides us, widow Landry and Father Nadeau."

"Maybe we should send for Father Nadeau."

"I'll speak to your father about it."

And *mère* Cormier went out, wiping her hands on her apron. A few minutes later, the black mare was hitched up.

Around four o'clock, a little before train time, the entire family was outside, taking in the last warm rays of the May sun. They were rocking in the big swings on the side veranda, out of the wind, except for Elise who had gone up to her room. Father Nadeau arrived in a hurry. They explained the events to him from all possible angles, twice being better than once. All the theories made at noon were examined one by one.

"I don't understand it," said *mère* Cormier, "we treated him well here. We gave him everything we could! Not a word of thanks, nothing, he disappeared like a thief!"

"That's what makes me think he had to leave in a hurry," the priest explained. "I know him well enough; he's not a heartless man! If he disappeared so quickly without a word, something must have happened. But don't worry, we'll find out sooner or later."

But despite all the priest's good words, *mère* Cormier was very eager to get angry.

"You can't trust those people! That type is always ready to run off like a thief in the night!"

"Don't speak so harshly, *mère* Cormier," the priest gently urged. "He still hasn't done anything wrong."

"Nothing wrong? Go ask my Elise who's been crying up in her room since this morning!"

"How's that again?" asked the priest.

"Just like that, for no good reason. She started crying at dinner, then she went up to her room. We've been listening to her sniffle all afternoon."

"What's wrong with her?"

"It's simple enough: he bewitched my Elise! I knew we shouldn't have trusted him! And he was so innocent looking the whole time!"

"Come now! Do you think so?"

"A mother has her intuition, Father Nadeau."

"Go get her. *I'll* speak to her."

A few minutes later, Elise appeared at the kitchen door, in a taffeta dress with lace cuffs, looking very much like a bereaved *grande dame* with her red-rimmed eyes and hastily put-up hair. The priest led her down the road. They walked through the dusty sunset.

"What's the matter, Elise?"

And she began crying again. The priest took her by the arm. He searched her eyes.

"Did something happen between you two?"

Elise shook her head with a sniffle.

"Then why are you crying?"

"Because I was starting to feel something for *monsieur* Nazaire."

"Is that why you're crying?"

"He's gone and he won't come back."

"He'll come back! And if he doesn't come back, you'll meet other young men! Your life has just begun, my child."

"I'm going to wait for him until the end of my days," Elise said.

"No, my child. That would be a sin. If the Good Lord in His Infinite Wisdom decided to take him away from you, then no doubt it was for the good of everybody, for you and him in particular."

"But I don't want him to go!"

"Keep quiet," the priest cut her off. "You should have

never fallen for him like that. He's a good fellow, but a deserter all the same!"

Nazaire had been missing for a month. Nobody had gotten word from him.. About the third week of June, the hay was already high in the fields. Cormier and the other farmers in the area had hitched up their horses to the big mowers with the pointed teeth and they'd begun the first harvest as early as the last week in June. The season promised to be a good one.

But manpower was scarce. People had to help each other. Loads of hay were seen returning with women and girls perched on top, all red and sweaty. But some women had neither the time nor the strength to do these hard tasks themselves. So the remaining farmers in the parish, old men for the most part, managed to lend a hand where it was needed most.

They were in the fields at the first light of dawn. At noon, everywhere you saw little girls going off to bring food baskets to the men. Seven or eight of them would gather under a tall elm and take a nap after eating, never for very long because work called. Only half the day had passesd, and they were already exhausted. With age, they'd lost the habit of hard work. But when the weather was favourable, they had to keep on until sundown. You saw them coming back at twilight. They ate like horses, their elbows on the table, and it was all they could do not to fall asleep then and there, after the meal. They went up to bed, broken with fatigue, and the women sat out on the front steps when the nights were too hot.

Some of them had gotten into the habit of walking to the village at night. After supper they gathered under the church portico for the simple pleasure of being together, twice widowed, once by the boys who'd gone to war and again by the men who were already asleep.

They sat in rows on the steps of the church portico to comment on the news from near and distant places. And the priest led them like a choirmaster.

"I read it in the paper this morning," he said. "It seems the

105

poor Parisians are in terrible danger. They're fleeing the capital of France by the hundreds—what am I saying?—by the thousands to avoid the bombing. They say there are endless convoys on the roads. They put everything they can in carts, furniture, mattresses especially, with the women and children on top, and they pull these carts themselves because the horses have disappeared a long time ago. They go into the fields or the woods. So you see," the priest summed up, "there are people in a much worse state than we are. Just about all of us have some relation in the war, a husband, a son or a cousin. But we still have our houses. Nobody bothers us in our houses and the harvest promises to be a good one. We don't lack for food. Think of the people in the cities who are rationed."

"That's all very fine," replied an old woman, "but what if the war comes here?"

"The war will never come here," the priest explained. "That's impossible."

"They say the Germans invented a cannon that can shoot a hundred miles!"

"Listen, Madame Beauséjour, there's a lot more than one hundred miles separating us from France!"

"I know there's more than a hundred miles in the sea, I'm no fool, but they can always come in their boats! If the Good Lord allowed the poor people over there to be punished for their sins, that could very well happen to us too!"

"We could even expiate other people's sins!"

"Keep quiet!" the priest cut them short. "Do you think that all those who are suffering now in the world are expiating sins they've committed? Never forget that God first tries those he loves."

"It's always the poor people that pay for the sins of the rich!"

"But who among us has a clean conscience?" asked Father Nadeau. "Who? Remember the parable of the adulterous woman. Let he who is without sin cast the first stone!"

But Madame Mercier changed the subject of conversation.

"I'm telling you, my daughter-in-law read it to me from

the paper. They say they have a cannon that can shoot a hundred miles. Incredible! As if the people in Montreal could shoot at us, right here!"

"It's called the Big Bertha," Geneviève Desrosiers announced triumphantly. "I know, it's the Big Bertha. That's how they baptized their cannon. I'd like to see that."

"You'd like it less if you were in the shoes of those unfortunate Frenchmen," Father Nadeau answered severely. "Imagine that you're sleeping quietly in your bed and suddenly the house falls down on you! It's terrible! And the most terrible thing of all is that they can't predict it. Before, during the day, the big cannon claimed fewer victims, that's understandable. People didn't stay in their houses. But now they fire in the middle of the night. You go to sleep and you never wake up. That's why you have to stay up and always be ready."

"If I were French, I wouldn't stay in Paris," said Madame Lambert. "I'd go to the country with my children, to somewhere where there weren't any Germans. There must still be some places they haven't gotten to."

"In any case," the priest cut them short, "if it continues, soon there won't be any more France. And then it will be England's turn."

"I knew it," repeated Madame Beauséjour, "I knew it: the war will be a long one. I foresaw it. But do you know who is going to stop their war? Our own brave soldiers who've gone off to the front! Good thing we have them!"

"Not like the others," said an anonymous voice, "the others who hid instead of going to defend us!"

"We mustn't judge them!" Father Nadeau asserted. "They're our brothers and no doubt they have their reasons for acting as they do."

"If it were up to me," said fat Madame Saint-Cyr, "they would have gone to war a long time ago!"

And silence fell under the porch of the church of Saint-Elphège. Madame Beauséjour, Madame Lambert, Geneviève Desrosiers and Madame Saint-Cyr suddenly find themselves in the fields in the middle of the afternoon. Each of them is working on her own and suddenly they hear a terrible sound. Big Bertha has just hit François Pépin's house with his eleven children inside. Or else this: it's July. It hasn't rained for almost two weeks. Everybody has gone together, one Thursday morning, to Mass for the fruits of the earth. And at the moment of the elevation, at the very instant the priest raises the Host over his head, the roof of the church crumbles. The people are twisted in the wreckage. Big Bertha has struck Saint-Elphège once more!

Nazaire had disappeared once again, without sending word to anybody, leaving people at a loss: Cormier the farmer and his family, especially Elise, Father Nadeau and widow Landry.

"But we treated him like one of our own children, Christ on a çrutch!" thundered Cormier. "A fine life, taking it easy in the hay, safe as can be! He ate well, he chewed the fat with us and had a good pipe every evening at sun-down. What more could you ask for?"

But Nazaire had quite simply disappeared. The Cormiers had done their haying. They'd had two fine harvests, then they'd worked here and there to lend a hand to those who couldn't do everything themselves. They rose early, they sweated, they went to bed early. They went to Mass in the village Sunday morning and afterward, by special permission from the priest, they put on their overalls again and returned to the fields. No rest on the Lord's Day. It was war and they were fighting it in their own way, battling against time.

Madame Cormier and her daughters spent endless hours in the big garden behind the house: potatoes as far as the eye could see, onions, turnips and cabbages. Enough to get through the winter, counting the two pigs and the chickens.

"Christ on a crutch!" Cormier the farmer exclaimed. "We're not rich but at least we can say we don't lack for anything! Considering we've already gotten through winter on a dime!"

And summer was beginning to weigh heavy. The cattails were bending in the ditch near the house and the corn was turning yellow in the fields. The autumn promised to be a mild one.

Elise's heart had not mended. She languished like a soul in purgatory.

"We know," her mother told her, "he might not be such a bad fellow, but considering the circumstances, it's hardly the time to fall in love with him! My poor daughter! Your Nazaire isn't master of his fate. He has to hide away like a thief. Try not to think about it. Forget him. You'll meet other young fellows from around here!"

That's what she thought! It happened early one September morning. The youngest of the Cormier daughters went to feed the chickens behind the house. She went around the back, already starting to call, Chick! Chick! Chick! She came to the henhouse and ran right into Nazaire who was in the middle of swallowing down a raw egg, his eyes sunk in their sockets, his beard black, his hair standing up on his head. A real *coureur des bois* who hadn't eaten for several days. She stood frozen there before him, her seed pan in her hands, her head to one side.

"Don't be afraid, it's me, Nazaire."

"I knew who you were."

"I won't stay long. Go tell them I'm here."

The girl ran off.

A few minutes later they all had their elbows on the oilcloth in the summer kitchen. They were watching Nazaire eat. Now his plate was empty. His chin was in his hands and it looked as though he was going to fall asleep. A long silence.

Finally, he explained, "I was nervous for no good reason. I couldn't stand it any more, in darkness all the time, in the hay. When you came to tell me the soldiers had come back, I saw the whole thing all at once in my head. I saw them there in the yard. I was so sure of it I went out carefully to take a look. Of course there was nobody there but I kept wondering all the same! I couldn't tell any more if what there was in my head was true or if my eyes were really seeing it. It was like I was crazy, you understand? So I didn't take any chances. The two boys were by the stable. I put everything right into a sack, my things, then I ran toward the woodlot."

109

"Christ on a crutch! Where did you go then?"

"I walked straight ahead like a beggar, with my sack on my back. I went past the woods then I came to the fields on the fifth concession. I kept walking for a long time. All the time I had the image of my hole coming back to me and it was worse than hell. I saw the soldiers searching everywhere and sticking in their pitchforks. In the end, I imagined they were devils with little pointed horns. I tell you I was walking at a good clip. I crossed the river and then I got lost in a big forest."

"Christ on a crutch! Where did you spend the summer?"

"I'd just as soon not tell you. But there's one thing I can say: where I was, I didn't eat my fill every day. I didn't always sleep as much as I needed to either. Now that you know all that, it's about time I leave. I didn't come back to stay. I was passing by and I said to myself that maybe it would be polite to come say hello and thank you for everything you did for me."

"Don't even think of it!" Cormier the farmer thundered. "We found you and we're keeping you! And where do you plan on going anyway? Winter's coming on!"

"I don't know yet."

"You're going to stay here, nice and peaceful, you hear me? And if you ever get the idea of running away again, *I'm* going to come looking for you, Christ on a crutch!"

At the end of the table, Elise smiled, her eyes closed.

Once again, it was time to prepare for winter. In Canada, it's always the same: you work like slaves six months of the year to be able to survive the other six months. You work to be able to feed the animals in winter. It's been like that since the time of the first settlers, but back then, on top of it all, there was the cloud of war casting a shadow over the countryside.

Nazaire said, "I'm not spending another winter in darkness in the hay. It's simple enough: I wouldn't be able to stand it!"

So they looked for another arrangement. They had the stable and the attic left. It wasn't convenient in the stable. They chose the attic.

110

"Easy to see why," Cormier the farmer explained. "If anything happened, all alone in the stable, you couldn't defend yourself. If the soldiers came, we wouldn't be there to divert their attention. But here in the attic, before they could find you, we'd have time to stall them or warn you so you could escape."

Besides, it wasn't the attic proper they were talking about, but the kneewall closet under the eaves. They decided it would be warmer than the real attic. The kneewall closet is where the sloping roof meets the floor of the second storey. There's a little wall the length of the rooms behind which a long, narrow corridor runs.

That's where it was, where people kept broken chairs, old newspapers, worn clothes, schoolbooks and cracked cauldrons. In the country, people don't throw anything away. They put everything that has outlived its usefulness in the kneewall closet.

It was by far the most comfortable hide-out Nazaire had had since he left his father's house in Nicolet. Old newspapers to stretch out on or to read from time to time. A grey blanket and, best of all, by leaving the little door half-open, he could hear the murmur of conversation downstairs in the kitchen.

He was like a chicken in its egg listening to the hens in the henhouse. A chicken that's so comfortable it doesn't have the slightest desire to break out of its shell.

Nazaire began hibernating for the winter. The border between wakefulness and sleep had faded. Everything melted into the same dream. They treated him like a king: three times a day Elise brought him up his meals and took away his chamber pot. Nazaire was ashamed but what else could he do?

Three times a day, then, the deserter waited impatiently for her velvet tread on the stairway. Elise bent over him through the little door and passed him his platter. Then she sat down on the floor. There they were, side by side, talking quietly to each other.

Elise was rather tall, thin, with a timid smile. Her hands were a little reddened by the housework and the chores around the farm, but Nazaire imagined they were soft. And one fine day her hands inadvertently touched him as she took back the

111

platter. Other times it happened as she leaned over to fold his blanket or take away the chamber pot. The two of them shivered every time. They gave each other long looks, without saying a word. One evening, at supper time, Nazaire quite simply took Elise's hands in his and lifted them to his lips.

"That's to thank you for all you've done for me."

But Elise had understood quite another thing.

One other time Nazaire said to her, "If it wasn't for the war, *mademoiselle* Elise, I'd be your beau. I'd come after supper, I'd knock on your door, you'd come and open it, I'd say good evening to you and we'd go into the living room where we could spend the evening together. It would be like that, every evening of the week. That's what I dream about all day in here."

Elise answered him in her softest voice, "It's the same for me, *monsieur* Nazaire. But I figure I'm lucky enough to be able to come see you like this three times a day."

"I'm like a patient," Nazaire said, laughing. "When the war is over, I'll be cured."

"And then will you come spend the evening in the living room?"

"For sure! If that's your heart's desire!"

Elise's feelings toward Nazaire were an open secret around the house. Her brothers teased her about it, her father discussed it in a gruff voice and her mother never stopped advising her to take a thousand and one precautions. But Elise finally overcame their resistance and hesitation, and Nazaire was allowed to descend from his hide-out after supper.

He began by going out to get a breath of fresh air for a few minutes, smoking a pipe with the Cormier boys, then he and Elise went into the living room. They were never completely alone, of course. That wasn't done back in those days. The father, mother, a brother or a sister had to stay with them at all times.

It was the middle of the war, on the edge of another winter, and the two young folks were already beginning to talk of the future—especially Elise. Nazaire was more reticent.

"It's not the time to talk about that, *mademoiselle* Elise," he said. "I don't even know what's going to happen to me when their war is over—if it's ever over! I've been hiding like a mole for almost a year now!"

"Don't talk like that, *monsieur* Nazaire."

"But it's the truth, pure and simple. And you know I've never been a very sentimental sort. I don't know how to talk to girls very well."

"You do to me."

Elise moved closer until her skirts touched the rough cloth of Nazaire's pants. And the evening flowed like honey. Around nine o'clock, Nazaire went back to his hiding-place.

Then again the geese began forming their big Vs in the sky. You heard them at dawn and sunset when they returned to settle onto the fields behind the Cormiers' house to spend the night. Immense formations, one, two hundred geese. Under the eaves, Nazaire plugged his ears to keep from hearing them.

There are limits to what a man can endure. And Nazaire was enduring, no doubt about that. By the time he was twenty years old he'd already been acquainted with a feeling most people flee like the plague, that they sometimes manage to avoid all their life: the feeling of solitude.

It was, in fact, a strange war Nazaire was fighting within himself. Lying on his old newspapers, he let pictures roll past in his mind. The little boy he once was, on the beaches of Port Saint-François. The rocking horse from one of his first New Year's mornings. His bicycle, Blanchard the foreman at his father's factory and the fishing expeditions in the Monteux. The images streamed past. Nazaire retained one and turned it this way and that. What would have happened if he hadn't put his hand on the branch and if it hadn't broken? He wouldn't have fallen into the water ... And what if Eugène hadn't been there ...?

Widow Landry, Father Nadeau, Cormier the farmer—and Elise. Nazaire came to believe he would live hidden away until the end of his days, and the thought did not entirely displease

113

A little before noon bells began ringing all at once in all the cities and towns in Canada. Of course Nazaire only heard the little tinny bell of the Saint-Elphège church, but he'd been told later that bells had rung everywhere at the same time.

People rushed outside into the sunlight, children ran to hide in their mothers' skirts, men dropped their hammers or pitchforks, women forgot their soup on the fire. The bells were bringing the news that the war was over.

Nobody had believed it at first. They'd needed to hear it over and over again. A telegram had arrived at the Nicolet station. A man returning from Drummondville had heard the news there. Another had received a message from his sister who lived in Bon-Conseil. And little by little, the truth had taken shape: the war was over!

Nazaire had gone out to join the others in the Cormiers' yard. They were all there, throwing their tuques into the air and dancing in a circle. Suddenly they stopped. They looked each other in the eye, grabbed each other by the shoulders, burst out laughing and began shouting again, The war is over!

The sun was shining and the weather wasn't too cold for an eleventh of November. It was a good sign: the war was over and winter wouldn't be too harsh. Around three o'clock in the afternoon Father Nadeau arrived. His horse was in a lather.

"The war is over, my friends!"

And the Cormier family kneeled down outside in the yard, on the patches of hardened snow, to say a prayer with the priest.

People were riding by on the road like on a Sunday, people from both the village and the country. They went from house to house. They stopped everywhere like during the *guignolée*. The war is over!

They saw Nazaire and asked, Who's that fellow? But they didn't need to hear the answer to understand. *Père* Cormier said, He's a young man who's going to spend the winter with us. And the people went off without asking any more questions.

But Nazaire, he was asking himself a few questions in spite of the celebration. He said to himself, The war's over for them but not for me! What's going to happen to *me*? They're going to

114

want to punish me for not having gone to war. They're going to put me in prison. I'll have to stay hidden. It's going to take a good six months before this business is settled. The war isn't over for us deserters!

He edged away on his own toward the back of the yard. He sat down on a log near the door of the woodshed and lit himself a pipe. He smoked, his head down.

And Elise, she'd taken a few steps in his direction and stopped. In her hand, she was holding her apron that she'd taken off but hadn't found the time to put down before leaving the house. She stared at her feet. Nobody was paying any attention to them.

They were all busy laughing and talking together. They were already talking about the war in the past tense. They said, Do you remember? Some of them were as proud as if they'd personally won the war. They said, I knew we were bound to win it! I knew it! If I'd been the right age, I would have gone and it wouldn't have lasted as long, that's for sure! We would have won that war quicker! Anyway, it's our soldiers who did it, that's for sure. Us *Canadiens*, we're not cowards and we've got guts!

Elise and Nazaire faced each other without saying a word. They'd been there a while when Jos Levasseur called to them, "Hey, you lovebirds, you're not celebrating?"

Elise came close enough to take Nazaire's hands in hers. In a low voice, she said, "The war is over, Nazaire."

"Not for everybody."

And Elise ran into the kitchen, crying.

Then, as if the war hadn't wrought enough havoc, people began dying. Especially big men and the ones we thought were the strongest. It started with Jos Leblanc. He came to the village, to the general store, in his checked shirt, his cap crosswise on his head. He needed a pipe for his stove. He said to Madame Camiré, I don't feel right today, I must be catching a cold. And Madame Camiré answered, Keep warm!

The next morning he was dead. It was more or less the same

for Michel Boulanger and widow Sinclair. One of them, little Bussières, held out longer than the others. Three days writhing on his bed. In the end his skin was all black, that's what they said. People began realizing it was no joke. They quickly understood it was a sickness you could catch, a contagious sickness. They began to avoid each other. They went out of their way to keep from meeting, from talking, especially from touching.

Notices were published in the newspapers. You could read it in black and white: there was no remedy against it. The sickness had been brought back home by the soldiers who'd contracted it on the battlefields. They called it the Spanish flu.

No remedy against this evil that had come from across the ocean. Cleanliness equals health, so said the newspapers. People washed, they took care of themselves as best they could, they made an effort to go to bed early with their caps pushed down on their heads and their nightdresses tightly wrapped around their bodies. What more could they do?

Every morning around eleven o'clock, you saw a cart go by, heading toward the village. There was a corpse in it. Every day it was more or less the same. In the country around Saint-Elphège, there was just about one death a day. What could be done?

They brought the deceased in front of the church, the priest came out under the portico, blessed him, threw three drops of holy water and that was it. They hurried to bury him. The man who did this job, big Desfossés, had already been banished from the parish because of his numerous vices. At the time of the Spanish flu, it was even worse: they ran him out with the help of a horse whip. But the sickness left him alone.

Children were dying too. Children of all ages, nine months, fifteen months, two years, four years. Later, when it had passed, the families had little white stone sheep set up over their graves. The cemetery became a regular pasture with little white sheep grazing in the shadow of the tombstones.

The autumn of 1918 was even more tragic for Canadians than the four years of war that had gone before. People said to each other, Will our misery never end? What could we have him. I'm like a monk, he said to himself. A monk who's nice and warm, well fed and loved by the daughter of the master of the house. He figured his lot wasn't so miserable after all. He was even beginning to develop a taste for it.

Elise surrounded him with smiles and the early mornings were cozy. He did his best to turn her a few compliments and the two of them had even begun saying *tu* to each other.

Father and Mother Cormier had grown accustomed to this routine too. Of course it wasn't what they had had in mind for their daughter, but it wasn't so bad either. She could have fallen for a village ne'er-do-well, while Nazaire was almost like one of their boys. They could keep an eye on him, in any case. That was reassuring.

One morning at the beginning of November, the eleventh to be exact, Nazaire heard shouts down below. He thought at first an accident had happened. He closed the little door, but as he listened, he realized they were shouts of joy. *Mère* Cormier began singing *La Marseillaise*. The daughters must have been dancing; you could hear their steps on the linoleum. Without knowing why, Nazaire began to shout too. Then Elise hurried up to explain things to him.

Even Father Nadeau had no answers. God's ways are mysterious, he said. And everybody understood he couldn't answer either. But he performed his duties as best he could, Father Nadeau did, going from one house to the next, comforting the sick and administering to the dying. They fought with a rage never before witnessed. They must have gazed upon death from close up, disguised as a witch, with her great sickle over her shoulder, bending over their beds, to struggle so much. But nobody ever found out. Once they'd reached that point, they couldn't speak.

When you're ninety years old, like old Madame Lalancette, you die without much of a struggle. You live your life, then your candle goes out. But at the beginning of the winter of 1918, men in the prime of life were dying. People who'd managed to survive the war, who'd gone to the front and come back safe and sound, only to die stupidly in their beds of a Spanish sickness. The women and children mourned. When the sickness entered a house, it could just as well carry off three or four members of the family and leave a six-month-old baby all alone in this world.

Other times it was the father and mother and two of their five children who passed away. That meant three little orphans nobody wanted because they knew they might be carrying the sickness. The nuns took them in. The convent had been turned into a hospital. The sick and dying were in the classrooms, with the desks and chairs piled up at the back; the orphans were kept in the part of the convent reserved for the nuns.

But other families weren't affected at all. Nobody knew exactly what could have been the reason; they didn't do any different than all the rest. They weren't the only ones who knew of the miracle cure: burning camphor on the stove. Besides, nobody really knew what to think any more because death struck those who burned camphor in their houses just like those who didn't. People were astonished too that the Good Lord came to claim the most virtuous and most wicked alike.

There was a man who wasn't religious at all, who lived all alone like an animal in a shack he'd built for himself at the end of Bellerose's property. Nobody knew his name but they called him Ti-bras because one of his arms was shorter than the other. He didn't have any family and he'd never worked. He earned his living doing odd jobs like weeding a garden or sawing up a tree. Mostly he lived off charity. When he'd reached the bottom of his purse, he'd come knocking at the back door of the convent and the nuns would give him a basket of food. You saw him less in the autumn and winter; he came to the village about once a week. Madame Camiré from the general store thought about him, because she hadn't seen him show up from time to time in the circle of old men who would gather around the coal stove.

She began to say, "I don't know what's happened. Nobody sees Ti-bras any more."

A few of them went to take a look in his shack. As you might expect he was dead, frozen stiff on his bed. He'd left an almost illegible note on the table: I will the money under my mattress to my daughter Ernestine in Montreal. People were amazed. Nobody knew Ti-bras had a daughter; they'd never heard of her.

Under the mattress, they found a thousand dollars in crisp hundred dollar bills. Quite a sum for those days! And before he died, Ti-bras must have raised himself to add a sentence to his last will and testament. He'd written, even more illegibly, at the bottom of the little scrap of white paper: I don't want no priest. The women of the village took advantage of the occasion to declare that Ti-bras must have died in terrible pain, and that he'd glimpsed, at the very moment he passed over to the other side, what awaited him in hell, since they found his face all twisted.

The Christmas holiday wasn't celebrated with much fervour that year, even less so than during the war. Nobody even knew if they'd be among the living the next day. No plans were made. People survived, limiting their movements and emotions. There was no talk of going off on foot through the snow to cut down a pine tree in the forest, bringing it back all frozen into the kitchen, decorating it with coloured paper chains and setting candles on it. In their anxiety, fathers and mothers had forgotten to make wooden trucks for the boys, a new dress for the girls and a fine rocking horse for the baby of the family.

There was no midnight Mass or New Year's celebration. No Epiphany dinner either, with the pea and the bean in the cake to choose the king and queen of the party. People didn't visit each other in the customary way. They were too afraid of catching the sickness. They burned camphor on the stove and went out as little as possible. There were no more family or friends. There were just people who were afraid.

The dangerous time was not completely over. The war had ended, that was true, but the harsh cold of January and the Spanish flu did not still all passions. The hunt for deserters was not finished. People who'd lost a father, a son or an intended to the war bore a grudge against them for their actions. You read in the newspapers that the Parliament in Ottawa was thinking of declaring an amnesty, but in the meantime, soldiers were still roaming the countryside.

The question had been debated back and forth around the oilcloth at Cormier the farmer's house. Nazaire was sitting at the end, like a condemned man.

"How can you trust anybody? Christ on a crutch! All it takes is one bad apple to spoil the whole barrel! So many people saw you the other day that maybe it's not smart for you to stay here. No use pushing your luck!"

They decided that Nazaire would return to widow Landry's house in Notre-Dame de Pierreville. Father Nadeau agreed with that. And Nazaire let himself be led, tired of struggling.

The day of his departure, he had a final conversation with Elise. She was in her Sunday best, her hair tied up in a chignon, and she had put on her beautiful taffeta dress with the lace cuffs. The two of them were alone in the living room. Elise was sniffling and she clasped her little white handkerchief in her hand.

"Don't cry," Nazaire said, "don't cry!"

That only succeeded in tightening Elise's throat.

"Don't cry," Nazaire repeated, "that's the way life is. The war is over for you but not for me. I've got to fight my war to the end. I'm condemned to hide because I'm a deserter! The others who came back from over there, in their fine khaki uniforms and their caps on the sides of their heads, they're the heroes now."

Now Elise was crying in earnest.

"But you knew I'd have to go away some day!" Nazaire went on. "You did your best not to think about it, but it had to happen anyway. And you shouldn't have ever let yourself have any feelings for me. Good catch, a deserter!"

"Don't talk like that!" Elise said through her tears.

Nazaire turned circles in the living room, nervous, his hands in the pockets of his homespun trousers.

"It's about time for me to go. Your father must have finished hitching up. Don't cry, I'll come back when it's over!"

"I know you won't come back! I just know it!"

"I'll come back and see you when it's over, I promise you."

"I know you won't come back!"

And Elise ran into the kitchen to cry in her mother's apron. Embarrassed, Nazaire followed her. He cleared his throat as he went into the kitchen, and stood there, upright, his hands in his pockets, in his felt boots, watching Elise and her mother. Finally he took his coat from the back of a chair, planted his cap on his head, picked up his pack that contained all his things and headed toward the door.

"Well, all right, I think it's time for me to go now. Good-bye, everybody! Don't cry, I don't deserve it! And thanks for everything you've done for me. Thanks again. Good-bye, then!"

And he went out without a second look, carefully closing the kitchen door behind him. Outside he found Cormier the farmer waiting for him in his wagon. It was beginning to snow thick and fast. A northwester was blowing.

"We'd better get a move on," said Cormier. "I don't feel like getting caught in the storm on the way back!"

Three weeks later, Nazaire was napping in his attic at the widow Landry's house. It was toward the end of January. He'd gotten used to the idea of spending another winter hidden, and he figured he wasn't too badly off.

The attic of widow Landry's little house was vast, with an unfinished wood floor, a criss-cross of beams for a ceiling and a round window at either end. Nazaire had a real bed in the middle of the room, with grey blankets and a little night table; every morning he found the water frozen in the big bowl. He dozed on and off all day and he slept all night.

One afternoon, he heard voices in the kitchen downstairs. He listened carefully, and finally he recognized Cormier the farmer and Father Nadeau. He wondered if something serious hadn't happened. He tried to understand what they were talking about; quickly he realized it was him.

Widow Landry explained that Nazaire spent all day in bed in the attic, and that he rarely came down; if he did it was in the evening to have a bowl of soup with her. But the two men questioned the widow more closely: Is Nazaire completely normal? Did she notice anything? No, he's like he always is. Did he say anything? The widow got worried: Did he do something wrong? Did he steal? Worse than that, answered Cormier the farmer. Christ on a crutch! Wait till I get my hands on him!

Nazaire heard them put the ladder under the trap door. A profound fear took hold of him. His arms and legs trembled and he retreated toward the back of the attic. He slipped on his heavy wool lumberjack shirt. He tried to get out through the little round window but the double pane resisted. They caught him there, in the act of trying to force the window.

"Mon Baptême de mécréant!" thundered Cormier the farmer. "Where do you think you're going?"

"Watch your language," Father Nadeau put in.

"Is that how you were going to escape?"

"I didn't know it was you. I was afraid."

"You didn't know it was us?"

"No. What's the matter?"

"Don't act innocent, *mon Calvaire!*"

Father Nadeau put his hand on Cormier's shoulder, but the farmer continued as if he hadn't noticed him.

"You dare ask us what's the matter, just like that! You're acting innocent!"

And, calming down, he went on in a softer voice, "Listen to me carefully, Nazaire. A sin you admit is a sin half forgiven. I didn't come here to cause trouble. So admit it!"

"I don't know what you're talking about!"

"Don't act innocent, Christ on a cross!" Cormier the farmer repeated in a loud voice. "I expected better than that from you!"

"But I'm telling you," Nazaire insisted, leaning against the window, "I don't know what you're talking about!"

And he held out his arms beseechingly. He spotted widow Landry's head at the top of the ladder. He searched for a sympathetic look from her, but the widow remained impassive.

Then Nazaire advanced straight toward them. He went as far as the bed, sat down with his hands on his knees and looked at them, his head bent, his eyes turned upward. They were standing before him.

"What's the matter?" Nazaire asked.

"I'll tell you what the matter is," thundered Cormier the farmer. "What the matter is, Christ on a cross, is that my daughter Elise is pregnant!"

"I didn't know that," Nazaire answered innocently.

Cormier growled between his teeth. "You didn't know, you didn't know! *Hostie de Calvaire!*"

"I didn't do anything. I'm telling you it's the truth, pure and simple! I didn't do anything!"

Father Nadeau leaned over him and put his hand on his shoulder. Nazaire jumped.

"Come now," said the priest, "you'd be better off admitting it."

"I have nothing to admit," Nazaire repeated. "I didn't do anything!"

And he shrugged off the priest's hand.

"Maybe you didn't do anything," shouted Cormier the farmer, "but my daughter is pregnant by you! She said so herself!"

Daylight faded. Suddenly it was darker in the attic.

"Light us some candles," asked the priest.

The widow searched through Nazaire's night table, then she stuck two candles onto chipped saucers. Their flames wavered in the cold air.

"Listen to me carefully, my boy," Cormier the farmer said suddenly in a calmer voice. "Listen to me carefully."

And he came and sat down by Nazaire on the bed, but without touching him. He went on, "Listen to me carefully. I came with good intentions. What you did is serious and you know it as well as I do. But things can always be arranged."

Nazaire stared outside. The cold night had brought its darkness. And the wind was whipping at the edge of the roof.

"I came here with good intentions," Cormier the farmer repeated. "Go half way too, and we might be able to get along. That's why I brought Father Nadeau with me."

Nazaire looked at him without a word, and Cormier continued, "Remember, a sin admitted is a sin half forgiven. A pregnant girl, and not married, that's serious!"

Then Cormier the farmer stirred up his own anger.

"And we took every precaution! I wonder when you ever found a way to do it! Christ on a cross! You abused our trust, and right under our nose on top of it!"

Nazaire lowered his head. The silence suddenly grew thick, and the cold made a nail pop in the roofing.

"A sin admitted is a sin half forgiven," Cormier the farmer repeated. "That's why I brought the priest with me. He'll hear your confession. After that I'll take you back to the house, then we'll find a way to get you married as quick as possible. Then we'll never say a word about it again, Christ on a crutch!"

And Nazaire kneeled at the foot of his bed in front of Father Nadeau, while Cormier the farmer and widow Landry retreated silently down the ladder, closing the trap door behind them.

Nazaire looked at Elise at the other end of the table, and she lowered her eyes. He looked at her and said to himself, I know I'm no expert in those things, but all the same they won't convince me that a woman can get pregnant from kissing a man! I know which end children are made from! So that means that Elise isn't pregnant by me or that she's not pregnant at all!

"... do you understand?" thundered Cormier the farmer.

"Excuse me," Nazaire said. "I was thinking of something else."

"Christ on a cross! Listen to me when I'm talking! Some son-in-law you'll make! Listen to me! The priest let me know that he managed to get dispensation from publishing two of the three banns. That cost me ten bucks, it did! Tomorrow, Sunday, he'll publish them at high mass. That way we'll be able to marry you next Saturday. The sooner the better!"

"Yes," Nazaire answered, lowering his head.

"Listen to me," Cormier the farmer thundered. "You're of age now, you're twenty-one. We sent for your baptism certificate from Nicolet. Your birthdate is marked on it. You're of age, you're free to do what you like. No need to ask your father. But we can always find a way to tell your parents if you like."

"I'd rather not," Nazaire answered.

"Whatever you like," said Cormier the farmer. "That's your business! Do what you like. But it's going to be my job to find you a witness."

And he left the kitchen pensively, his back bent ever so slightly. Mother Cormier took refuge at the corner of the stove. The lamplight picked out Elise and Nazaire in the centre of the kitchen. The girl started sobbing again. Then Nazaire stood up, came to her side and put his hand on her shoulder.

"Don't cry. You shouldn't cry before your wedding! I know that it's not a wedding like most but that doesn't matter! Don't cry. We'll find a way to make it beautiful anyway."

"You're not too angry at me?"

"I'm not in a position to be angry at anybody. I'm like a prisoner. To keep from being too miserable, I tell myself that everything that's happening to me must be for the best. I'm of age to get married now. And a pretty girl like you, well, you'd have to be crazy to turn up your nose on it. And I'm not crazy, you see? I'm a lot less crazy than people think. And if I'm getting married to you, it's because I want to."

And he walked away, leaving Elise to ruminate on her lie. Mother Cormier busied herself with her pots.

They were married the following Saturday. Fat Ernest Gagnon served as Nazaire's witness. A very simple ceremony, at ten o'clock. In the church there were only the Cormier family and a few devoted souls who never miss anything. Elise's mother had sewn her a beautiful long dress made of pink silk. The devout onlookers understood immediately: when the bride isn't wearing white, it's a forced marriage.

The Létourneau spinster played the harmonium. Nazaire

125

and Elise said yes, looking each other in the eye, and finally Elise smiled. Obviously Nazaire didn't have any money to buy a ring for his intended. They'd agreed to take the one that belonged to the late grandmother Cormier, and Elise turned it lovingly around her finger.

After the ceremony, they went straight back to the house. There was a beautiful white tablecloth on the table, the linen one for the Holidays, covered with fresh fruit. There were pine branches pinned to the cloth at the edges of the table. The Cormier boys twisted their heads left and right in their starched collars. Slapping his son-in-law on the back, Father Cormier thundered, "You're part of the family now. Come sit next to me!"

They threw back a little glass of *caribou*, then another. They ate a chicken that Cormier had killed the day before. For dessert, Mother Cormier brought out the big, two-tiered wedding cake that she'd prepared on the sly. On top was a little paper bird and these words carefully cut out from a piece of cardboard: LONG LIFE.

The day passed in a gentle euphoria but as soon as darkness settled in, around four o'clock, the father and his two sons changed clothes to go do their chores in the stable.

"The animals give the orders around here!"

When they came back, they ate again, just a bite, then they lit their pipes, sitting in front of the oven door. Nazaire had untied the tie Cormier had lent him, a fine black tie for special occasions.

Then the father spoke. "You, Nazaire, tomorrow you're going to go back to widow Landry's house while you wait for everything to be fixed. You've attracted plenty of attention the last while, and I don't want my son-in-law to get arrested by the soldiers the day after his wedding. For tonight, you'll sleep upstairs, in the guest room. I'm dead on my feet. A day like this is more tiring than a whole week of work. Come along, old girl! Goodnight, everybody! And go to bed, you too, children."

Alone with Elise, Nazaire put more wood in the stove. He took his wife's hands in his and he said, "You told everybody you

126

were pregnant by me. Let's find a way to show them we're not fools. Come to bed."

Things began coming to an end. That's the way it is in this life. Everything ends up coming to an end, even the worst. Nazaire returned to his attic in widow Landry's house in Notre-Dame. He'd put on his homespun trousers and his lumberjack shirt again; he'd gone back to his long empty days at the window. He'd just gotten married and already he was separated from his wife!

Things were coming to an end. People had stopped dying. The Spanish flu had passed, you heard about it less and less as the winter set in. People said, The germ's frozen. It couldn't put up with our climate. It's understandable, a germ from over there!

And the war was clearly over too. Those who'd been to the other side had returned. Some told horrible stories night after night. Others kept silent, not a word: I'd rather not talk about it! But in either case, the heroism of the French Canadians and the glorious battles in which they'd fought were conjured up. They'd seen France, England, Belgium and Holland. So it really was true what you learned in geography books!

Wood was burning in the two-tiered stoves in the kitchens. Coal was glowing red in the furnaces in the basements. It was the heart of winter. The air had become as brittle as glass and the silence was deep. In his attic, Nazaire was shivering like a drowned rat. February, cold enough to freeze the breath in your lungs. In an unheated attic!

He spent his days wrapped up in his blankets. His nose and ears were frozen. And he thought of his wife, whom he'd known but one single night.

Again he pictured her long white nightdress, he heard the springs of the bed creaking under the weight of their bodies. Most of all he remembered the burning sensation he'd felt when he'd drawn her near and kissed her. He'd stared into the darkness before him and said aloud, You are my wife! Elise had answered Yes, then, more softly, A wife must obey her husband. And Nazaire had overcome his final moment of hesitation. He knew what he had to do now. Besides, he wanted it very badly.

In the darkness, Elise had closed her eyes. Their two bodies had grown warm under the blankets. Finally, Nazaire put his hand under her nightdress and brushed her breasts. A fire was burning in his chest and parching his throat. He pushed up Elise's nightdress to her hips and lay down on her. Now with his eyes closed in the darkness, he began seeking his way.

But when the next morning dawned, he'd laced his felt boots and climbed into *père* Cormier's sleigh. Their honeymoon was already over.

As the days went by, they had to face the facts: Elise wasn't pregnant. She tried to explain it: Maybe I was wrong; maybe I lost it the time I fell on the ice coming back from the henhouse. It hurt me down in my stomach for no good reason.

And to console her, her mother said, "Don't worry. If you're like your mother, you'll get pregnant the minute you see your man!"

And he was beginning to lose his endurance in his attic in Notre-Dame de Pierreville. He paced back and forth like a condemned man. He couldn't stand it any more. One morning he went down to the kitchen and announced he was leaving. He said to widow Landry, You've been like a mother to me. Never in my life could I repay you. I'll never forget.

Widow Landry wiped her hands on her apron before kissing him on both cheeks.

And he left with a fisherman named Paul-Hus who, as it turned out, had some business to do over by Saint-Elphège. The fisherman left him a good mile from Cormier the farmer's house and Nazaire continued along on foot. He wanted to see his wife. His feet were so frozen he couldn't feel them any more. He wanted to be all alone with his wife, but he reminded himself it still wouldn't be possible. He was walking at a good clip. He wanted to be like a husband with his wife; he couldn't stand his bachelor's life any more. He walked into the kitchen. *Mère* Cormier was prowling around the stove as usual. She was alone.

"Sit down, my boy. Come put your feet on the oven door."
Nazaire asked, "How are you? I've come to see my wife."

"She's in the henhouse."

And she was just coming back with her younger sister. She stopped in the doorway when she saw Nazaire.

"Close the door, we're not rich enough to heat God's heaven!"

She ran to him and threw her arms around his neck. They both laughed like children.

"I missed you," said Elise.

"Our misery is coming to an end," answered Nazaire.

"Take me with you."

"Our misery is coming to an end," Nazaire repeated. "I'm going to Nicolet to fix things. There's a limit to everything! They can't hang me, after all. It won't take long. I'll fix it all and come back and get you. Then we'll be like husband and wife. Both of us together in our house. I'll buy you a sewing machine. Our misery is coming to an end. We've suffered enough as it is. We'll have children like everybody else. Beautiful little children who'll look like you. Our good times are beginning, I'm telling you!"

Through the window, the sun sent a frozen ray of light.

"You won't hear the end of this!" Nazaire's father said. "It wasn't enough for you to go and hide out like a thief, you had to come back married on top of it."

They were in his father's office at the factory. Nazaire reached Nicolet about nine o'clock and went directly there. He sat down on the little swivel stool that the furniture designer used, and he turned one way and then the other. His father stared at him from under his green visor.

"Just what came over you?"

And he shook his head, waiting for the answer. His beard and hair had turned white in the space of a year. His breath was a little shorter, it seemed. A tired man.

"And what are you going to do now?"

129

"First I'm going to have to find a way to settle this business. I can't stay hidden until the end of time. It's no life, especially when you're married!"

Nazaire's father jumped at the words.

"Who's your wife?"

"The daughter of a farmer in Saint-Elphège where I was hiding."

"When are you going to show her to us, since you didn't even have it in you to invite us to your wedding?"

"That's not it ... it just wasn't possible."

"How come?"

"I'll bring her here to Nicolet as soon as I've settled this business."

"Here you are, ready to fall into Courchesne the notary's hands!"

"I don't see any other way."

"Let me do it at least. Go back quietly to the house and try not to cause your mother too much pain when you tell her you got married without saying anything to us. I'm going to see the notary."

And Nazaire's father stood up. He put on his broad-brimmed felt hat, his wool overcoat and his kid gloves. He moved toward the door, then he turned to his son.

"Now that you're married, you're going to have to earn your living and your wife's too. You have responsibilities now. That might do you good, besides."

He hesitated and turned the door handle in his hand.

"I'm ready to give you one last chance. You can work here with me, in the factory, taking care of some contracts and helping me in the main office. And as it turns out, I just bought a little house for not too much down river. You know, *père* Charland's old house. I said to myself I'd fix it up a little, then I could sell it. If you're prepared to do everything yourself, to avoid the costs, you can stay there as long as necessary. There's no hurry."

Nazaire opened his mouth to answer. His father had already gone.

The next morning it was Nazaire's turn to go to Cour-

chesne the notary's office. Black suit and strong smell of cigars.
The notary gave him a seat and took a good long look at him,
rubbing his hands together.

"Do you want a cigar?"

"No thank you."

"So you've come back, just like that, eh, Nazaire? Can you
tell me where you were hiding?"

"I'd just as soon not talk about it."

"As you like. But you do know these things are
complicated?"

"I know. But there still must be a way."

"Of course, everything can always be arranged. It's going
to take a little time, and you can't live on thin air, you know. But
your father told me not to skimp on the means."

"That's right. I'll be reimbursing my father later."

"That's your business. It doesn't concern me."

And the notary rested his arms on the blotter. He leaned
toward Nazaire, speaking in a low voice with a strong smell of
cigars.

"You'll do what I tell you to and everything will be
arranged. It might take a little time before everything is completely official, but in the meantime, nobody will come and
bother you."

"Do you think I can stay here in Nicolet and start working
again?"

"Act as if nothing happened. If somebody asks you any
questions, don't answer. If something seems a little strange to
you, let me know. I'll take care of everything. I'll send the
account to your father."

"You're very kind."

And Nazaire signed a few papers and forms that the notary
held out to him.

Once he was outside, Nazaire started to breathe again like
a prisoner who's just been freed. He was amazed that nothing
had changed, the milkman's horse stopped at the same place,
the same clothes on the line and the two little old men turning
the corner. He walked down the main street as far as the

Restaurant Central and suddenly he felt like going inside. Just to see people. And maybe to show them he was back too. It smelled like French fries.

"Well, if it isn't Nazaire! Where have you been?"

"You know as well as I do!"

"Don't get me wrong! We're just kidding!"

"Hello, Nazaire!" said *père* Lupien, the owner of the establishment. "You've changed! You might say the war made a man out of you!"

... Then I woke up on the roof. Wrapped in my blanket, I'd spent the night changing hide-outs like Nazaire, freezing and keeping watch like Nazaire. I'd been like Nazaire all night. I'd been Nazaire and I was coming back to the world, as he had when he'd returned to Nicolet. A stranger in his own town! Starting everything over! Experiencing everything!

I understood later. I understood for myself when I secretly returned to our house in Vermont. I had a wife too, in Montreal. A wife and a little girl.

It was early morning, a little before the light comes up completely, when you begin to make out the shapes of the trees.

On the porch roof that night, I'd become so much like Nazaire that, without even realizing it, later I'd taken the same steps he had. Hiding to keep from going to war in my own way.

I looked down. They were like conspirators around the fireplace. They were talking in low voices. My brother Germain had a blanket over his shoulders like an Indian. All of them were still there around my father, but the fire had gone out.

"We'd better catch an hour or two of sleep," my father said, "if we want to find our deserter today."

I shivered. I would have given anything to keep them from finding him. I wrapped my blanket around my shoulders. All the dampness of the early morning was on me.

"We'll find that deserter of ours," said my father, standing up. "In the meantime, we'd better catch an hour or two of sleep."

They went into the house. Some of them picked up the empty beer cans that were lying on the lawn, then they all went in. I was all alone, watching the fog settle into the hollow of the valley. All alone.

PART THREE

They must not find him! I didn't know why but I was absolutely sure of it! Watching Jay peak pierce the fog had convinced me.

Now, at twenty-five, a deserter myself, a wife and child left behind in Montreal, I know I understood infinitely more back in those days, at fourteen, than I could have realized.

Already I knew that Nazaire hadn't gone off to hide like a coward because my father had talked about the Depression and the war. Already I guessed that Nazaire had gone off to do battle. He had gone to do battle against the forces in us that are a hundred times stronger than the hurricanes and all the storms there are on the sea. Forces you don't control, that you must fight against to survive. Forces that, even today at twenty-five, I couldn't name but I know intimately.

It's amazing when you think about it. I knew all these things vaguely at fourteen. Ten years later, it was as if having lived them made them more confusing.

I did the same as the day before. I followed the men. But this time nobody had said "No kids." I could have walked in the open at their side, but I preferred to keep my distance like before.

Germain, Willy, my sister Rita, Sheriff O'Connor of course, Cy Bradley too, but not his sons, Fred Dennisson, Sam, Max, Lennie and Bill Donohue. A dozen, more or less.

"The guys from the State Police will be here later today," the sheriff said, his hands hooked in his belt. "They're going to meet us up at the top. But let's hurry and find him before they get here. I don't want to look like some kind of hopeless case."

We walked in silence, most likely because nobody had slept much the night before. Everybody was a little numb, a little rocky. They were all keeping to themselves. It was like in the winter when you've stayed too long by the stove. Everybody was stuck inside himself.

We must have walked a good two hours. Without really realizing it, we picked up a little road that we call Long Trail around here. It cuts through the woods on the mountain and climbs right to the top of Jay Peak. A logging road. A road that curves like a snake and bends back on itself from time to time to circle a big rock or border a stream. And it goes straight up.

I'd gone a few times on Long Trail but never alone, because it's a dangerous place, they say. It's true it's easy to get lost on it. What happened is that, in time, people opened up other roads that branch off from Long Trail and disappear into the forest. There's no way of knowing, of course. Everywhere are the same trees, the same underbrush, the same brown light. You're walking, you come to a fork, the two roads are the same. One of them wanders through the forest or along a high plateau and the other goes on being the real Long Trail.

As the crow flies, from our house to the top of Jay Peak, it must take five or six hours by foot. But if you got lost and went to the end of the roads that lead nowhere, you could walk for a couple of days.

My father said, "Maybe he followed Long Trail."

"Maybe."

And we walked along single file on Long Trail, happy to be in the shade because the day promised to be a hot one, and with the fatigue from the day before and the sleepless night, nobody felt like climbing on all fours up some impossible slope or crawling through the bushes.

Then we reached a fork. My father said, "We're going to have to go to the end of each of these little roads. But let's make sure we don't get lost too."

The sheriff grumbled, "You better! I don't want to get involved in a massive search!"

A car or truck went by from time to time. We felt like stopping them and climbing in. Nobody had the strength to walk for hours along the little branches of Long Trail. But that was what we did. We went to the end of the first little road, then we came back to where we started. We walked for another half hour, then we found ourselves again at a fork that we followed to the end. There we reached a place where some cutting had been done. We sat down on the stumps. We were as quiet as if we were in church. The sun was just above us; it was almost noon already. The men began smoking, yawning, talking among themselves. We didn't feel like going further.

My sister Rita said to my father, "You didn't tell us much about Elise."

"She was a real beauty," my father answered.

The men began eating the food they'd brought. Big egg sandwiches with mayonnaise. Bottles of Coke and thermoses of coffee. Then they stretched out for a nap. They closed their eyes but they didn't sleep. They listened to my father talk about Elise.

Paul arrived in the pick-up truck.

"Are you there? I've been looking for you everywhere."

"Anything new?"

"No, I was just coming by to see. I've been driving everywhere since morning, in places you'd never think of. I stopped the truck to listen. Nothing. I didn't hear a thing. If he's not dead, he's well hidden!"

They must not find him! When Paul left, I climbed in the pick-up with him. I was standing up in back. We were driving on Long Trail, covered with pine needles, in the direction of Jay Peak.

I knew they must not find him! It had started the night before on the porch roof. I was listening to my father without knowing that what I was hearing was important. It must have come from the breeze. It must have been because of the stars too. And the fire below and the men sitting around it. Then this morning my father had spoken once again, with all of us sitting around him on the stumps in the clearing.

First it happened between my father and me. Like a lamp passed from hand to hand to light the way. A lamp that would grow more luminous as it went forward.

Then it had become something between Nazaire and me. I know it's difficult to explain but, at that age, I'd already learned there were two sorts of truth: the inside truth and the outside truth. That's why you don't always understand why people act one way or another: because you only know the outside truth.

It was that way for Nazaire. Everybody who was there on the mountain, searching for him, knew only his outside truth. But without really wanting to, in the course of the night and the morning, my father had revealed a little of Nazaire's inside truth to us. Actually, he'd spoken only of the outside truth, but in a way that he'd left the door to the inside half opened. And I had glimpsed Nazaire's truth from the roof. And because of that I knew they must not find him. Because they'd understood nothing of his inside truth. And that could put Nazaire in grave danger. Today, I have proof that the intuition I had at fourteen about Nazaire was right: I acted as he had later on.

I was standing in the back of Paul's pick-up. We were driving slowly. The trees bent down as we passed. I had a good view of the underbrush and I kept my eyes open. And all the mountain forest was like a presence that spoke to me, not with words of course, but to my heart.

The road was rising steeply. The wind washed my face and the smells reached me with a force of their own. It was about two o'clock in the afternoon. It was warm but we had a breeze as we drove. There were insects flying past me, and sometimes they brushed my face. And all that surrounded me whispered Nazaire's inside truth. A love story. A story for a twenty-five-year-old draft dodger. A story so alive it was as if Nazaire himself had told it to me. As if I had heard him tell me, In those days, I wore homespun trousers, handsome suspenders with POLICE

137

written on them and a grey cap. I smoked my pipe with the bowl
pointing down to impress the girls. You couldn't say I ran after
them, not at all, but I did cause quite a stir when I strolled down
main street. I walked at a good clip on the wooden sidewalk, my
hands in my pockets, and I whistled *Vive la Canadienne!* when I
passed by the girls. In those days the girls were pretty. They wore
long dresses down to the ground with pinafores on top, and
sometimes a big straw hat. On Sundays, during the summer,
either to go to Mass or simply for a stroll, they carried lace
umbrellas in their hands. Beautiful umbrellas in all the colours
of the rainbow. Imagine it: the wagons pulling up before the
church, the ladies stepping down, holding up their skirts in one
hand, their umbrella in the other. It was enough to make you
smoke your pipe with the bowl pointing down! And in those
days the weather was fine; it was warm all summer. The girls
went for a stroll on Sunday afternoons on the main street. Two
by two, three by three, or in larger groups, always accompanied
by their mother or an aunt. Us boys were moved to the ends of
the earth. We wanted to speak to them, walk by their side, offer
them an arm, spin them fine yarns, show we had some wits about
us. But we didn't dare because of the mothers and the formida-
ble aunts. That's why we liked to go fishing so much. We went
fishing in the Monteux. As you know, you can't talk when you're
fishing. So we were quiet and we thought things over. We
thought about the girls. That made us want to organize a picnic.
From time to time we succeeded. We got together, ten boys or so,
and as many girls. We went to the riverside. That was in the days
of the big wicker baskets, beautiful white tablecloths and excursions in red rowboats on the river. You saw umbrellas there
too, umbrellas of every colour. You even saw—but not very
often—the big, full bathing suits. Us boys had striped trunks.
We swam across the river to impress the girls and came back out
of breath. We lay down on the wool blankets. We ate what there
was on the white tablecloth, and we were full of clever things to
say. The girls would tell us, Stop making us laugh or we'll
suffocate to death! Sometimes we were lucky enough, when we
turned around quickly, to brush a tuft of hair with our nose. It

smelled like sweet honey. And we took their hand too, to help them jump over a brook or climb a fence. We were all about the same age. We didn't know much but we were happy. We'd never been out of Nicolet but we talked to the girls all about the wide world. We told them things we'd read in the newspaper. We said they were as elegant as the ladies of Paris. That made them blush because flirting was forbidden in those days. And, to put it frankly, Paris was like Sodom and Gomorrah. We'd never been out of Nicolet but we dreamed of taking them on endless voyages around the globe. That was our own way of dreaming we were rich and strong.

We were like blades of grass caressed by the wind. We were happy for no good reason and we didn't ask ourselves where it could have come from. We weren't the type to ask troublesome questions. We built fires on the beach at Port Saint-François, enormous fires that must have been seen all the way from Trois-Rivières. We rode on our bicycles with balloon tires. We went to play baseball against the fellows from Pierreville. There was a handcar at the station. We borrowed it, six of us climbed on top and we pumped the big arm that made the little machine roll down the rails at top speed. We arrived in Pierreville around seven o'clock and had time to play our nine innings before dark. We won almost all the time. Without fail, it ended in a brawl. And we had canoes too. Cedar strip canoes with good canvas stretched on top, and painted green. We crossed the river to Pointe-du-Lac. We said we were Indians on our way to kidnap the Pointe-du-Lac girls. But the people there had been warned we were coming and we didn't find a soul. That didn't matter; we were in a good mood anyway. On the way back, once we reached the river channel, we capsized the canoes on purpose and went in swimming. We swam back practically the rest of the way, pushing the canoes in front of us. We went hunting in the autumn. We froze in our blinds but we ended up killing fifteen, twenty, thirty ducks, even if it was against the law to bring back that many. We ate them with pork and beans. Our mothers even made jellied duck in Mason jars. Then came the time of the Holidays. There were parties almost every evening. We didn't turn up our noses on the *caribou!* We danced until we dropped from fatigue on the floor. We spent all our time having fun. And we were great tricksters too. At my father's cottage in Port Saint-François, we let fireflies loose in the girls' room. We put toads in the drawers, we untied pinafores of course and we cried wolf more often than we needed to. It was our own way of showing we were happy to be alive. We didn't ask ourselves any questions, not at all! We were careless the way youth is. You have to understand that: we didn't have much in those days but that didn't keep us from being the happiest fellows in the world. I was lucky because I worked in my father's factory, lucky enough to be able to disappear weekdays, when everybody else was at work. I worked as fast as I could to save a nice afternoon for myself. I liked to be alone a lot too. I always was like that. There was nothing sad about it. I was fine all alone. When I felt that desire coming over me, I went walking in the forests that used to be all around Nicolet in those days. You could walk through them for whole days without meeting a soul. And then there was the river. I had all of that to myself. I walked along the river and it was as if each breath was a mouthful of blackberry wine. In the end I was nearly drunk. I felt my blood flowing through all the veins in my body. My head was as light as a balloon, and at the same time my heart was full to overflowing. I liked that feeling a lot: my head empty and my heart full. I couldn't take another step. I lay down on my back, my arms wide open, and I watched the clouds pass by. You can't imagine everything I learned watching the clouds. They're like a window, and you can see the other side through that window. I wouldn't say that I understood everything I saw—that wouldn't be true—but my feeling was strong enough to guess a good bit of it. It might last one hour or two. I closed my eyes, then I opened them. I was still back in the same place, yet everything had had the time to change. That made me think. I said to myself, The world is infinitely great and the earth is turning in space and I'm lying on the globe turning with it. Then I said to myself, We're

all as one, the plants, the animals and men. We are the flower of
the earth. We come into the world, we grow, we blossom, we die
and we turn into fertilizer. It's the same for men, for plants and
for animals. Only us humans, with our little something extra, we
know that. I've never been very knowledgeable about the Good
Lord's business. But I did say to myself *that's* what the Creator
must have given us: the responsibility of knowing all that in
place of those who weren't able to. In those moments I felt
overcome by a great love for everything on the face of the earth.
I turned my head to speak to the blades of grass next to me. I
sang songs to the birds passing overhead. I said things to the fish
that must have been in the river, and I wanted to caress the fur of
all the wild beasts. I ended up falling asleep most of the time.
When I came back to the house, you can imagine that I didn't
feel like talking. That's why people took it into their heads that I
was sad. I wasn't sad. I'd never been so happy. And when I think
about it, that's how my love story begins.

The woman I loved, I loved her and her alone more than all the
plants, all the stars and all the animals. There was nothing else
but her in the world, can you understand that? Even though
things weren't looking up when I met her. Those were the worst
years of my life. I'd just as well not talk about it. It's something
I'd like to erase from my memory. All I can say is this: I was like a
dead man for an entire year. Like a dead man who'd kept the use
of his mind. And it's worse than hell, I can tell you that! You're
dead, you see everything, but you're helpless. You'd like to keep
somebody from doing something wrong, to stay the hand of
somebody who's about to kill another, to run your hand through
the grey hair of a mother crying all alone by her stove. No. You
see all that but you're helpless. Then little by little you begin to
forget the difference between what's happening outside and
what's happening in your head. It's all frozen together in the
same block, like in autumn when the cold moves in. Everything
is all together, the grass, the clay, the earth, the sand, the water,
the tree, the bit of wood, the shirt forgotten in the field, the

pencil dropped from a pocket, the rock, the swallow's nest. It's all together, frozen in a single icy block. You forget the difference between dreams and reality. But understand this: the dream is a hundred times worse than the reality in those times. And the reality is no laughing matter either. You're hidden in a hole, waiting for the war to finish. It's terrible, but it's really not too bad after all. What's really terrible is when you begin to imagine what could have happened to others. You don't even know if they were called to the front or not. It's all because you don't know anything that the dream becomes a nightmare. You begin by imagining Hervé Bourdon with his big boots running between the barbed wire, bent double, as the bullets rip into his body. When he makes it to our trenches there's nothing left: his arms torn away, his legs cut down, his head blown off, his trunk opened up. There's nothing left but a spent heart that stops beating in my hands. Or else Jeannot Proulx on a ship sinking in the middle of the sea. Kneeling on the bridge, he prays to the Virgin Mary. Or else Baptiste Métivier who goes off without a second thought to get provisions and steps on a mine. Understand me: I'm not saying this to you for the pleasure of telling war stories, but to make you see what sort of man I had become, hidden in the hay, when my love story began. I was so miserable my love story took shape without me even realizing it. I wasn't even able to understand the simple things in life any more. Not clever enough to realize it was no accident that *mademoiselle* Elise was coming to bring my food more often than was her turn. I thought she was pretty nice: she managed to stay with me a few minutes, to make sure I was comfortable, that I didn't need anything, to chew the fat with me. I was so cut off from this world that I didn't even notice her cheeks were red, that she kept smoothing her hair and stifling bursts of laughter. In another time, had it been like before, I wouldn't have done either of *those* things—I would have paid her a compliment. It wouldn't have taken me long before I would have given her a little peck on the cheek. I'd never been a great ladies' man, but still! Only then, since I'd been living hidden in the hay, I couldn't see or hear a thing. That's why Elise started it all. She must have begun loving me little by little. Those things are like grass fires: once they've begun, you can't control them any more. Elise loved me and she sent me messages to tell me so. But I was deaf and blind, as if I'd been paralyzed. But she was patient. She must have said to herself that she had all the time in the world, that surely I'd end up noticing. That I couldn't go away, in any case. And she wasn't the type to hurry things, either. My Elise didn't have very much experience in those matters. A country girl who'd never been to the village for anything else but Sunday Mass. Only Elise had intuition, like all women. Right away she set out knitting me a net with bits of wool, tufts of hair and smiles. I still didn't see anything, and it was obvious why: I was deader than a corpse. And maybe if I'd responded right away to her little messages, it would have led to nothing more than a wartime love. But instead, things were taking a very different turn. But Elise, who thought she'd have all the time in the world to finish her net and snare me in it, was caught unawares. The war ended as unexpectedly as it had begun. I was about to steal away without a word, like a thief, just as I'd come. Elise went into a panic: her net wasn't ready. She'd caught me by only one foot, at the last minute. She acted out of desperation. She loved me too much to let me leave. That's why she said she was pregnant by me. I knew very well it wasn't true. I was taken completely by surprise. I wanted to get angry, only at the same time I'd come to see that I loved Elise. I didn't say a word and we got married, just like that. That's when everything turned beautiful all of a sudden, like when it's been stormy for a week, and one fine morning the sun comes shining onto your bed. All of a sudden I began to live again. My father had just bought a little house down river from Nicolet, a little outside of town. It was at a bend in the road, on a bluff covered with lilacs, on the riverbank. That's where we settled in. Then we took out the paint and the wallpaper, and the hammer and nails too. I was still amazed to discover I had a wife. I'd left Nicolet like a thief, still a boy, and I came back married, like a man. That gave me strength for the work. And I didn't want to think that Elise had said she was pregnant by me. It burned me like fire. Anyway, just looking at

her made shivers come over me. It was like that for the first
months: one good day, one bad day, one day saying to myself
that Elise had lied to me, another day loving her without a
second thought. But it was beautiful anyway. We painted, we
papered, we fixed our house, as I told you. That's what cured me
once and for all. That's how the summer passed, and then we
settled in for our first winter. You'll never convince me that a
man and woman working together to ready their house for the
winter can be unhappy! Impossible! When you bring in an
armful of wood, you're already feeling warm all over. When
you're caulking the windows, you already feel as you do on early
winter mornings, too cozy in your bed to get up. It was those
early mornings that reconciled us completely, Elise and I. It was
simple enough: we were feeling too good to feel bad! We were in
our long flannel nightdresses. Daylight hadn't risen yet, just a
soft blue glow. We were snuggled up against each other, the
eiderdown on top, the tips of our noses frozen and our hearts
warm. I opened one eye; Elise was watching me with a smile. I
was so close I could smell the scent of her breath warmed by
sleep. The scent of a person is a great way to heal the breach.
You can't feel somebody's breathing and be angry at the same
time. It's impossible. I smelled Elise's scent and I smiled back at
her. She said, You're not asleep? I answered, Neither are you!
We laughed. I moved even closer to her, I slipped my arm
beneath her, where it's warm and soft. I held her close to me and
I said to her, You make the dawn come up. When you open your
eyes, the sun rises. It's not hard to imagine that at times like that,
you don't think about the lie at the beginning. It was at those
times that we would wipe away the lie. It was simple enough:
there was nothing to do but turn the lie into truth. That wasn't
hard. We only had to lift up our nightdresses to wipe away the
lie. And that's what we did. But plenty of times it came over me,
I would sit in a chair by the stove without saying a word for a
good hour. It was as if I'd gone back to my hole in spite of myself.
But Elise was patient. She waited for me to come back to her. We
ate without a word. After supper I took my place again by the
stove, then a little later we went to bed. It could even last for
days on end.

Elise was patient. One fine morning we awoke in the blue dawn and we wiped away the lie. The day I had awaited had come. It was beautiful like never before. It was in April, one of those warm days when you begin to want to unbutton your coat. The snow was melting in the sun before your very eyes. There were puddles of water everywhere in the street. It was a Saturday. We went out for a walk together, like lovers, on the down river road. We heard the crows. That's when Elise told me she was pregnant.

Standing in the back of the pick-up truck, shivers ran down my spine. More than anything, they must not find Nazaire! I was the only one who knew!

It was as if I had the taste of Nazaire's breath in my own mouth. They must not find him!

We reached a major turn-off. There was a whole crowd there. Two trucks and a car marked Vermont State Police. Men in brown uniforms, with boots and clubs at their sides. They were talking into walkie-talkies and mysterious voices answered them. There must have been others on the mountain! Shivers ran down my spine.

Paul had gotten out and he was looking at a military map spread out on the hood of the car. Five or six of them were bent over the map. They were dividing the mountain into sectors: section three, four and five. Then they talked into the walkie-talkies: three point five miles north, to the summit! They must not find him!

Paul said to the commander, "I'm going up to the top in the pick-up. The road ends about a quarter mile before the summit. After that there's a little footpath that goes up. I'll wait for you there."

We went off again at top speed. I took my place in back again and I hung on because of the bumps. My head was spinning. Nazaire's breath continued to tell me of my life to come.

You've got to take good care of a pregnant woman! I said to

my Elise. No more washing the floor, I'll look after it! Take good care of yourself! Don't think of anything but yourself! Stay in bed in the morning! Read your missal or open a novel. If you run out, I'll go get you some more at the library. Books you've never read. Or knit quietly. Now's the time to prepare the baby's things! Make him a little hat and some angora wool socks.

I said that to my Elise, then I kissed her tenderly and went off to work in the factory, sitting straight on my bicycle with the balloon tires, singing at the top of my lungs. At noon when I came back to the house, I was in for a shock: I found Elise at the stove. I told her, Don't worry about that, I'll make dinner! She burst out laughing and answered, I'm pregnant, I'm not sick!

On Saturday, I got down on my hands and knees and washed the kitchen linoleum with the big red and white flowered pattern. After that, we both went for a walk, not too far, not too fast, to keep from tiring her. We started to say there were three of us, Elise and me and the baby. Elise walked with her hands clasped in front of her, and little by little the circle grew wider. In the end it was as if she wanted to take the earth in her arms and press it to her stomach.

We'd prepared the child's room long ahead of time. Downstairs, near the kitchen, because it was warmer. With new curtains and a wicker cradle with a tulle canopy on top, a white one because we didn't know if it was going to be a boy or a girl. A cupboard too, full of diapers and quilts, swaddling clothes for a newborn, with bonnets and thick wool socks too.

In October, Elise began to feel heavy and wanted the time to pass more quickly. She was impatient. In the evening we sat in the kitchen by the stove. We left the door half open to see the fire. Elise said to me, I want it to be a boy. A boy so I can see what you looked like when you were little. Afterwards I'll make myself a little girl for me. And I answered, It doesn't matter, Elise, make us a beautiful healthy baby. But Elise repeated, I'd like it if it was a boy. Boys have less pain in life. I answered that it wasn't true, that boys had as hard a life as girls. In the end, I didn't care if it was a girl or a boy.

November, then the beginning of December. The doctor

had said it was due around the fifteenth of December. We began counting days, then we counted hours. But it was a crazy winter. Everything froze hard as a rock for a few days, then it started raining. The earth suffered from it. Elise was silent now. She got up at night because she couldn't sleep any more. She rocked herself by the stove.

It happened during the night between Saturday and Sunday. I ran to get Madame Beaulieu. Elise was breathing hard. A little later she cried out and bit the sheet. They laid out a big oil cloth on the bed, then a sheet that was old but still clean. Towels too, close by. They tied a thick rope between the two bedposts so Elise could pull on it. Then I ran off like crazy to Nicolet to bring back my mother and Doctor Smith.

They left me alone in the living room. I heard Elise crying. I heard steps, voices, cries, the sound of things being moved around, the basin on the night table. There was a long silence then everybody cried out at once. Another silence, then a child's wail. Through the wall I heard, It's a girl. It was too beautiful; my heart was overflowing. I began to cry softly. I heard somebody opening the bedroom door. I couldn't stand it any more. I ran out and went to hide in the woodshed to cry. A little girl! A little girl who came into the world because of Elise and me! I had a knot as big as a fist in my throat. I was crying because a little girl had come into the world in my house and she would look like us, like Elise and me.

Then I went back in with an armful of wood. Everybody was looking for me. I said, Now's no time to run out of wood! Then I hurried into the room. I walked on the tips of my toes like in a church. Elise's eyes were closed. She was smiling. The little girl was in her cradle at the foot of the bed. I was silent. It was as if I was coming into the world a second time.

They must not find Nazaire, no matter what! Especially not the State Police. Neither my father nor my brothers nor the neighbours either. And I had to look after that. Look after Nazaire.

The pick-up climbed the last curves before the end of the

road. I felt myself growing like a tree. I clenched my teeth. I could almost touch the wind. I was closer to heaven. Time had begun to melt. A block.

Nazaire's mustache in the leaves of the trees, his suspenders, his house before me on the road, Elise's hands in the wind and little Jeanne's hair. I held onto the pick-up to keep from falling because my heart was beating so hard. My heart was beating with enough strength to keep Nazaire, Elise and little Jeanne alive. Yet Elise and little Jeanne had stopped drawing breath long ago. Perhaps Elise had been right: did boys have less pain in life?

It happened one evening at twilight, in the early morning. In Nazaire's house, in the 1930s in Nicolet. First little Jeanne, then Elise. Carried off one after the other.

Elise's and little Jeanne's breath in my chest!

A child of three, sick in her bed. The lamp, the window, day and night, the doctor and everything beginning again. Time passes like drawing in breath. When time was weary, it ceased and little Jeanne lost her breath. Her father and mother had sunk down at her bedside. On her knees, Elise read the prayer for the dead from her missal, a prayer she had never read until then and did not understand very well. A prayer that asks us to rejoice, that speaks of eternal life, most of all of the resurrection. Elise looked at her little girl dead in her bed and she read aloud the words of the resurrection. Jeanne had no more use for breathing. Her hair was so soft and her hands were crossed on her chest. Her eyes closed. A rosary between her fingers. Three years old. She never learned to say her rosary. And her hair was so soft.

Then the man came to the house with his briefcase stuffed with documents. He looked at the child on the bed, he looked at the father, he looked at the mother; then he held out a paper to sign. Then he signed it himself. Jeanne's death was written there on the paper. Then another man came, then two more, then everybody in the neighbourhood. All coming to see the dead girl. A three-year-old child! Ten people in the kitchen. They're drinking tea as they talk. It's hard to let them go! Jeanne is lying on her bed in the next room. Yes, it's hard to let them go! What can you do? You'll have more children, at your age! No, never! I won't have any more! The Good Lord gave me a child, he took her away from me, may his Holy Will be done but I won't have any more! I'd rather stay like this, all alone, sitting with my Elise, my hands on my knees, waiting. Don't try to understand. Wait.

Time. Like in my time. Like in my hole. Like all my life. The breathing of time. The breath of time. The taste of time in my mouth. I tasted time but I couldn't choke it down. I tasted time and I didn't like it.

It's because you never accepted it. You always rebelled. You always fought against what was stronger than you. When they told you to go to war, you answered No! When they told you your little Jeanne's time had passed, you answered No! You rebelled against what was stronger than you: time.

Ten years later. Hair already grey. The same mustache, but grey, the same movements in the same house. Once again, the neighbours. Elise is on the bed. It is her turn to be swallowed up by time. Nazaire is there like before, on his knees. All alone this time.

It's always the same thing. Something always happens. You were twenty, you were happy, you spent your days fishing in the Monteux, war broke out, you had to hide. It ended up coming to an end, you climbed out of your hole, you married the most beautiful woman in the world, you had a child, the child died. Again you were forced back into your hole. You let time pass a little, you began living again, then your wife died. But still ...

But still you too had a taste for it. Like everybody else. A taste you couldn't name. A taste for eternity!

They're around Elise's bed. They tell you, Cheer up. She's better off where she is. She suffered so much. The Good Lord's ways are above us. But you don't answer. Never again will you speak; perhaps you will not hear either. Not the voice of the dead! Not the hymn for the dead! You will be all alone with your own breathing!

They just couldn't! Not that! And I was the one who would have to stop them. In the pick-up truck, we reached the place where the road ends. Paul had climbed out and was searching the area.

There are two paths. One climbs toward the summit and the other goes around the edge to weave down the other side of the mountain.

I knew what I had to do. I began running down the path that leads down the other slope of Jay Peak. I was running so hard the blood rose in my throat. I had Nazaire's knife in my hand, and now and then I stopped to slash a good piece off a branch. I ran like that for a good ten minutes, enough time to cut twenty notches on the branches, then I began shouting at the top of my lungs. I sat down and waited.

Paul arrived, trying to run, his leg stiff, a pained look on his face.

"Look, there are notches everywhere. He came by here. He went down the other side."

"Yeah, I saw them. I would have never thought he'd get this far. Poor old nut! You'd think he'd decided to walk back to Nicolet. Wait for me here! I'll go get the men at the bottom."

My heart was beating so hard I was afraid Paul would hear it. He disappeared down the end of the path and I began running like a madman through the brush, toward the summit. Just before you get to the top it opens out. There are no more trees, just bushes.

The summit is round. There's one final fold, then you're at the top. Nazaire was there, sitting upright, his shirt sleeves rolled up, looking straight ahead. I came near.

He must have heard me but he didn't turn his head. He simply said, "Is that you, Jean-François?"

Because I forgot to tell you, my name is Jean-François.

150